To Be Continued . . . .

volume one

. . . . Gordon j. h. Leenders

ECW Press

Published by ECW PRESS
2120 Queen Street East, Suite 200, Toronto, Ontario, Canada M4E 1E2

LIBRARY AND ARCHIVES CANADA CATALOGUING IN PUBLICATION

Leenders, Gordon j.h.
To be continued . . . / Gordon j.h. Leenders

ISBN 1-55022-668-1

I. Title

PS8573.E359T6 2005 C813'.6 C2004-907048-7

Editor: Jennifer Hale
Cover and Text Design: Tania Craan
Cover Image: © Matt Brasier, Masterfile
Typesetting: Wiesia Kolasinska
Printing: AGMV

This book is set in AGaramond

The publication of *To Be Continued* . . . has been generously supported by the Canada Council, the Ontario Arts Council, and the Government of Canada through the Book Publishing Industry Development Program. Canada

DISTRIBUTION
CANADA: Jaguar Book Group, 100 Armstrong Ave., Georgetown, ON L7G 5S4

PRINTED AND BOUND IN CANADA

To my new family:
Shannon and Mason
(and Brandi, our canine companion)

hold that thought

"I said I would do it when I was ready and now I'm ready . . . No, I won't . . . I don't care if he cries this time . . . Because this time it's different . . . Well, I'm sorry you don't — actually, just forget it. I'll get someone else to call . . . You will? Promise? I might have to hand the phone off to him if he doesn't believe me . . . I don't know. Just tell him it's a family emergency and you need me to come over right away. Okay? . . . Yeah. In half an hour. Thanks. Bye."

Claudia hit the END button on her Nokia cell phone and, after glancing at her watch and adjusting the strap on her leather sandals, continued walking north on Locke Street South, her eyes reflexively wandering into the various shops and cafés, occasionally pausing to peruse an outside menu or savour a piece of antique furniture or funky clothing in one of the window displays.

Oh, I just love this area, Claudia said to herself, slowing her pace in an effort to soak in the optimistic buzz swirling around her. She'd frequently commented to friends and acquaintances that Locke Street South in Hamilton was like a miniature version of the Beaches in Toronto or Rue St. Denis in Montreal — the sidewalks, especially during the summer months, continuously clogged with pedestrian traffic, a pulsing parade of freshly sun-kissed faces busily browsing boutiques, people-watching, devouring the daily newspaper, and/or gabbing excitedly over a café latte and a toasted spinach bagel.

Of course, I might have a slight bias, Claudia added, snatching a savoury sniff of chicory emanating from Locke Street Bakery and observing two pregnant women pushing identical three-wheeled baby strollers, the warm weather offering the mothers a chance to model the latest in summer maternity fashion.

The slight bias was derived from the fact that a considerable chunk of Claudia's familial history had its origins in the Locke Street South neighbourhood: her great-grandparents moved to Tuckett Street in the late 1800s; her grandparents had lived on Charlton Avenue; and her parents, married now for nearly forty years, met for the first time one morning at the Locke Street Library, promising each other a few hours later, after hopping a train on the TH&B (Toronto-Hamilton-Buffalo) Railway, to remain together forever.

Not only was this familial history responsible for Claudia being so enchanted by the Locke Street South neighbourhood, it was also why she believed it was her destiny to meet the man of her dreams here. And, undoubtedly, why, despite having just told her mother she intended to break up with him, she hadn't completely given up on Phillip.

"Is that you?" Phillip asked as she entered the apartment.

She'd been standing outside the apartment door for almost a minute, listening, hoping that if she waited just another few seconds she'd perhaps hear something — a paintbrush brushing, typewriter banging, guitar playing, pots and pans clanging — anything to indicate he was occupied. But there had been no such sounds. Claudia, her hand alternately reaching for and retreating from the doorknob, knew this could mean only one thing: that Phillip was alone with his thoughts, and the urgent phone call she'd received an hour ago meant that his thoughts had crystallized and were in need of an audience, a sounding board — a.k.a. Claudia.

Until last fall it was a role she enjoyed. Since then, however, she considered his thoughts to be more than mildly disturbing, not so much because of their subject matter, but because they were indications of a mind increasingly distant and separate from her own.

"Yeah, it's me," Claudia replied, closing the door, the smell of charcoal already invading her nostrils, making her slightly nauseous.

Their apartment used to smell of lilacs and vanilla and jasmine or any number of scented candles, prompting her friends to comment that it was like walking into The Body Shop or a Monet painting. Shortly before Christmas, however, Phillip became completely enchanted by Van Gogh's early work and began an apprenticeship in charcoal sketches. Claudia had thought (had hoped, actually) that by now he would've moved on, graduated to colours, his sketches becoming breezier, more playful, more floral, more Monet-like. But they hadn't. And now it seemed as though the apartment would forever smell like a coal mine.

"Where are you?" Claudia called out, stepping out of her sandals and placing them carefully in the hall closet.

"I'm in the studio," he said.

"I'll be right in," she replied.

Until a month ago, the "studio" had been their living room — a room in which Claudia had, after considerable personal expense, achieved a unique fusion of contrasting styles, tastefully blending antique and modern décor into a vibrant, yet harmonious tableau that her friends and family all agreed worked brilliantly. And then, one morning, she'd come home after working a double shift to discover Phillip had converted it into a Luddite-inspired artistic workshop, where the TV, computer, stereo, DVDs, and camcorder had been summarily replaced by a typewriter, a guitar, a pottery wheel, a drafting table, books, and an easel.

"You couldn't begin to imagine how I felt," she'd told her mother. "I was looking around with what must have been this stunned expression on my face, desperately hoping to find the host of some home renovation show or *Candid Camera* hiding somewhere, waiting to pop out and say, 'Surprise!' and ask me if I liked it."

But it was solely Phillip's idea. He told her he'd done it for them, that he wanted to create a space free of the detritus of modern living, a place that would preserve their mental environment. "Besides," he'd said, "you've been telling me since we met that you wanted to stop watching so much TV and learn how to play guitar and do pottery again. Well, here's your chance."

"But where did all *my* stuff go?" she'd asked, exasperated.

"I dropped it off at your mother's place," he'd replied, matter-of-factly, as though she'd asked him to do this, as though eviscerating the apartment without consulting her and getting rid of nearly all her furnishings and decorations was something she'd requested. Of course, her mother thought the incident was more than slightly fortuitous — and not without its advantages. "It'll make it that much easier for you to move out now. Providing you ever summon the courage to break up with him."

Her mother did not approve of the match.

Phillip was a __________ artist (select and insert any of the following modifiers):

a) struggling
b) brilliant
c) poor
d) narcissistic

It wasn't that her mother despised artists. She didn't. In fact, she admired them, especially aspiring artists like Phillip. She merely believed they made very poor partners and never let pass an opportunity to remind Claudia of this, regaling her with stories of their egotism, whims, neuroses, notorious instability, and the devastating effects these personality traits usually had on those who decided to be with them. Her mother's motto was, 'You don't date the artist, you buy his paintings.'

"I thought you said you'd be back at 1:00 p.m.?" Phillip said as Claudia entered the studio, his tone more curious than accusatory.

He was in the far corner of the studio (where her Templeton Settee from Pier 1 Imports used to be), sitting cross-legged on a large forest-green throw cushion, his head slumped forward in his hands, his thick dark hair spilling through his thin, pale fingers. He looked like a gloomy version of the Dalai Lama.

"There was an accident on the Queen Street access," Claudia replied, lying.

The truth was she was just parking her car in front of her grandparents old house on Charlton Avenue when he'd called, intent on going for a walk around the neighbourhood, longing to see it through her eyes again, unadulterated by Phillip's corruptive commentary, by his allegation of the area being contaminated by subscribers to J. Crew, The Gap, and L.L. Bean sipping over-priced cappuccinos while searching for the latest 'must-have' piece of antique décor.

"It took you almost an hour," he said, his tone and position unchanged.

"Yeah, I know. Everybody had to wait until the police and tow trucks got things sorted out," she replied, setting her leather trim clutch purse down on the drafting table and noticing that the T-shirt he was wearing, the one he'd found in Port Dover last summer, was now threadbare, a wash or two away from being thrown out. "Anyway, I'm back now," she said, sliding onto the drafting stool. "Is everything okay?"

"Not really," he replied. Then, a moment later, he sighed heavily and groaned. Twice.

Here we go, Claudia said to herself, knowing from past experience that this particular sigh-double-groan combination meant, 'I need another, more sincere-sounding inquiry before I'll tell you what's on my mind.'

She moved closer to Phillip, plunking down on the loveseat. Aside from the throw cushion, the loveseat was the only thing of hers that had survived 'the living room make-over,' as her mother now called it.

Claudia ran her left hand slowly across one of the arms of the loveseat, the soft, supple, slightly brushed fabric sending a sentimental spasm through her. She'd had it re-upholstered the day before moving in, using some material she told Phillip she'd picked up at a local second-hand store, but which her mother had actually ordered from an upscale fabric boutique in Montreal.

"Seriously, Phillip," Claudia said, doing her best to sound sincere. "What's up?"

After another sigh, Phillip raised his head slightly, his eyes momentarily wandering around the fringes of the studio before coming to rest on a spot somewhere near his bare feet.

"The GDP."

"The GDP?" Claudia replied, only slightly surprised. Phillip had been doing this quite frequently as of late, using obscure beginnings as a launching pad for his ever-expanding list of grievances. "You mean the Gross Domestic Product?"

Phillip nodded. "For as long as anyone can remember, the GDP has been trumpeted by economists, CEOs, and politicians as our main indicator of economic progress. According to them, as long as the GDP is going up, we have a strong, healthy economy and the country and everyone in it will prosper. Of course, what they don't tell you is that whenever there's an oil spill or a house fire or a car accident or a divorce or a forest being clear-cut or someone decides to fly an airplane into a building, *that's* when the GDP actually goes up. And that's because these sorts of things generate money. And so, the more house fires, car accidents, and 9/11s that happen, the better it is for the economy."

It was precisely this type of talk that had initially captivated Claudia. She'd grown weary of the men she normally dated; all established men in their late-thirties to mid-forties, it seemed as though their spontaneity, their joie de vivre — not to mention their honesty — had either ebbed considerably or been replaced by a veneer of professional cool. Certainly, they were knowledgeable; dressed impeccably for any occasion; could speak intelligently on investment portfolios, what wine to drink with a particular meal, and where to vacation; and, of course, could afford the wine, the dinner, and the vacation. But, aside from the pursuit of more luxury, they possessed very little passion — especially the unedited kind, the kind that shouted at you, spilled on you and, like a toppled glass of red wine on a white silk blouse, left permanent stains. That was Phillip; he left stains.

"Can you believe that?" he was now saying. "I mean, how psychotic do you have to be in order to design an economic system that actually *prospers* whenever a river gets polluted or someone gets killed in a car accident?"

Of course, it was also this type of talk — specifically the frequency of this type of talk — that was now driving Claudia away, that was responsible for creating the ever-widening gulf between them. Phillip rarely wanted to discuss anything but serious issues. Where before their conversations had contained elements of the trivial and the profound, the silly and the serious, nowadays there were very few moments when they just sat around discussing something silly or inconsequential. Everything had to be serious. With a capital 'S.'

Tears were now forming in Phillip's eyes.

Claudia edged forward slightly in her seat, "You know, Phillip, you're not responsible for this."

"Then who is?" he shot back, his voice starting to crack. "I mean, if everyone said that, where the hell would we . . ."

He didn't finish his sentence.

Claudia looked at him, closely, carefully scrutinizing his appearance. She found herself doing this often lately, trying to determine if he'd lost any weight, if he looked sleep deprived, if there was any discernible evidence of sickness. But he seemed fine. He had none of the telltale signs of depression — weight loss, sleeplessness, loss of interest in activities, suicidal ideation. In fact, if anything, he appeared healthier and more alive than when they'd first met.

■ ■ ■

It was the day Bush gave the order to attack Iraq. They were seated beside each other in the pre-boarding area of JFK Airport in New York, waiting for the same plane. He'd noticed the headlines on CNN and made her a bet.

"I'll bet you they don't find any weapons of mass destruction in Iraq. In fact, I'll bet you it comes out that Bush and Tony Blair manufactured evidence in order to get support for this war."

"What's the wager?" she'd asked.

"We stay together until they find the weapons."

"Deal."

The following day, during lunch at La Cantina, they'd laughed, remarking how ironic it was that they had to travel to another country to meet someone who lived in the same city.

"So, do you live around here?" he'd asked after their fourth coffee refill.

"Pretty close," she'd replied, nodding. "But I'm moving soon."

"Not out of the country, I hope."

She laughed. "No. Just to Locke Street."

"Really? You already have a place picked out?"

"Not yet. I just really love Locke Street."

"North or South side?"

"South side."

"I'm looking at a place on Locke Street South tomorrow."

"Oh my God, really? Where?"

"Above a place called The Vintage Garden Tea Room."

"In the Regent Apartments, right?"

"Yeah. How'd you know?"

"I just love that building."

Two weeks later, despite her mother's warnings, Claudia moved in with Phillip.

"Why on earth are you doing this, Claudia? You know virtually nothing about this man."

"Oh, mother. Stop being such a mother."

"Well, you don't. And I can't help it. I *am* your mother."

"I like him. A lot. He's different. He's intense. He's passionate."

"Well, just remember what Mr. Yeats said about passionate intensity."

"Easy on the drama, mother. Besides, you know I've always wanted to live on Locke Street ever since I was a kid. And now I can. You should be happy. I'm getting a great guy *and* a great apartment."

■ ■ ■

Phillip was now sobbing, his face once again submerged in his hands, the tears squeezing through his fingers, falling onto the throw cushion, spotting the fabric.

Instinctively, Claudia reached out to touch him, wanting to place her hand on his shoulder, maybe rub his neck (it was where he stored his tension), but she hesitated, recalling the last few moments of her conversation with her mother, how her mother refused to believe Claudia had the courage to break up with Phillip, telling Claudia that when it came down to it, Phillip would cry, Claudia would console him, and they'd stay together.

Withdrawing her hand, Claudia reached over and pulled a couple of tissues from the Kleenex box sitting on the nearby end table. Handing them to Phillip, she said, "Maybe it's time you —"

"What? Write another letter?" he snapped, tossing aside the tissues before angrily swiping away the tears with the back of his hand and glaring at her, his eyes suddenly soaked with rage. "A lot of good that's done."

In the past year or so he had written dozens of letters to various levels of the Canadian and U.S. government, as well as to the editors of numerous newspapers, magazines, and journals throughout North America — not one of which had been printed or made any discernible impact.

"I wasn't going to say that," Claudia said.

"Oh," he replied, his eyes softening, the rage dissipating. "What were you going to say?"

Claudia hesitated, her fingers now tracing the raised lettering on J.P. Fitzgerald's business card that she had just pulled from the front pocket of her suede skirt. She'd met J.P. at her ten-year reunion last week at the University of Toronto. He was the boyfriend of one of her old classmates and told Claudia he might be able to help. "Like my business card says, I specialise in providing viable solutions to postmodern-day dilemmas." Though he had no real qualifications to speak of, neither a degree nor any formal training as a counsellor, J.P. seemed like just the type of person who could understand Phillip.

"What I was going to say," Claudia said after a few moments, "was that maybe, um, I don't know, maybe it's time you saw someone."

"You mean a shrink?"

"Well, maybe not exactly a shrink. Maybe just someone you can talk to."

Phillip half-smiled, shaking his head. "It's going to require a lot more than a few conversations with someone to get me to feel better, Claudia."

"Then what will?"

Phillip sighed, running his fingers through his hair. "I don't know. Maybe if you knew someone capable of completely changing the world we live in."

Claudia's left hand spread out over the front of her skirt, alternately gripping and releasing the fabric, wrinkling the material. What the hell happened, she wondered. They used to be so good for each other, so in synch. She loved that he was interested in politics and world affairs — so was she. So was her entire family. She used to love going over to her parents' place every Sunday and having lively discussions during dinner. But all this changed when Phillip became too serious, too honest, and far too emotional to bring to dinner.

"When did all this become so important?" Claudia asked, slipping J.P.'s card back in her pocket.

"All what?"

"This. What you talk about nowadays."

"I don't know, it just did."

Claudia groaned.

"It's as though he kept it hidden from me," she'd told her mother. "Then, once we'd been living together for a while and he knew I really liked him, he started introducing it into our relationship."

"Your father was the same way," her mother said, laughing.

"He was?"

"For the first year of our relationship your father never farted. Not once. I thought I'd found the perfect man. The week after I accepted his proposal of marriage, however, he started farting. And he hasn't stopped since."

Passing gas was one thing, a full-blown personality change was quite another. Claudia's friends at work jokingly suggested Phillip may have suffered a brain injury, citing examples of persons who, although outwardly appearing the same, had become radically different people due to the damage to their brain.

Though Claudia was quite certain Phillip hadn't acquired a brain injury, she was equally certain that something had to account for such a radical change, for why he stopped eating any type of junk food, drinking coffee, dining out, and watching TV, and started eating only organic food, drinking herbal teas, cooking all his meals, reading books, writing letters to the government, and making impromptu speeches on anything from the war in Iraq to the dangers of refined sugars. There had to be some explanation for why he had become so serious; why, like the milk he now drank, his emotions had become so raw and unpasteurized.

Of course, the irony in all of this was that as difficult as these changes were for Claudia to stomach, as potentially problematic as she saw them to be, she wasn't asking Phillip to give them up; she merely wanted him to temper them. Just a little.

"You know," Claudia said, sliding slightly forward on the loveseat, "maybe it's not the world that has to change, but your view of the world that has to change."

"And what exactly is wrong with my view of the world?"

She shrugged. "I just wish you wouldn't see it as one big problem."

"I don't, Claudia. Really. I don't. But I also can't overlook the misery and ignorance and pain and greed in the world. I can't ignore the fact that there are thirty-five million cases of AIDS in Africa or that we've got just as many obese people as malnourished people in the world. And I especially can't ignore the fact that we've got the most inherently flawed economic system ever imagined and the vast majority of people aren't even the least bit concerned about it."

"Phillip, people are concerned."

"No, Claudia, people have the *appearance* of concern without the *reality* of being concerned. I don't know how many times I've been having a conversation with someone about something like poverty or homelessness or the environment or the incidence of obesity and they'll stand there giving me the appropriate facial expressions and verbal commentary of a quote-unquote, *concerned citizen*, but as soon as I leave, the person remains as detached and unaffected as before."

Claudia groaned, dropping her face into her hands.

"Hey, I'm not being this way to annoy you," Phillip said.

"Well, it does."

"I'm sorry. But this just feels right, you know? It feels like the real me."

"I liked the old you a lot more."

Phillip laughed. "Is that why it's been months since we've been to your parents' place for Sunday dinner?"

Claudia hesitated, debating whether or not to say what was really on her mind. Oh, the hell with it, she said to herself, before turning to Phillip and saying, "Do you have any idea what it's like to be around someone like you, when even the act of buying a certain type of bread is considered a crime? I mean, why do you have to be like this?"

"Like what?"

"Like how you are. Can't you just be a little more, I don't know, reasonable?"

Phillip smiled. "To quote your favourite playwright, Mr. George Bernard Shaw, 'The reasonable man insists on modelling himself after the world. The unreasonable man insists on modelling the world after himself. Therefore, all progress depends on the unreasonable man.'"

"Just because someone I like said it, doesn't make me feel any better, Phillip."

"Then what would?"

"If you changed. If you weren't so . . . *unreasonable*."

Phillip chuckled. "And just why should . . . no, forget it. Let's try something else. Let's say you're right and I do need to change — not only myself, but also my view of the world. How do you propose I go about doing this?"

"Are you asking me seriously?"

"Yes."

"I don't know," Claudia said, shrugging. "I mean, if you don't want to see someone you could, you could try, I mean, you could always take something."

Phillip gave her a look of disbelief. *"That's* your solution? To medicate me? Pop a few Soma tablets and I'll see things differently? Claudia, I'm not one of your patients."

He was referring to Claudia's job. She was a nurse in the psychiatric wing of St. Joseph's Hospital. Phillip used to jokingly refer to her as Nurse Ratched from *One Flew Over the Cuckoo's Nest.* In the last little while, however, as he became increasingly aware of the ever-expanding list of manufactured illnesses and diseases that could only be treated by costly drugs, the joking had been frequently replaced by cynicism.

"I don't necessarily mean taking Prozac or Paxil," Claudia said, haughtily, feeling slightly offended by his last comment. "I'm saying that maybe the occasional beer or glass of wine or some marijuana might help."

He smiled. "You're joking, right?"

"Well, didn't guys like Hemingway and Van Gogh drink or use drugs?"

"Yeah, they did. And look what happened to them."

Claudia sighed. "But doesn't it bother you that you're so upset all the time? Don't you think you'd feel better if you had something to take the edge off?"

"Claudia, I'm not looking for something to take the edge off. Stop trying to find a *cure* for the way I feel. I enjoy my emotions. I enjoy feeling depressed and sad and angry and frustrated and disillusioned every bit as much as I enjoy feeling happy and content and optimistic and lucky. I want to feel *all* my emotions. And if something makes me feel angry or sad or hopeful, I think it's only natural that I'm able to express the appropriate emotion. The last thing I'd want is to —"

"I feel like a tea. Would you like one?" Claudia asked softly, hoping to change the subject.

"The last thing I'd want is to be separated or detached from my emotions, to be on something that reduces or completely erases the way I should feel under the circumstances," Phillip said, ignoring her. "If someone is legitimately angry or depressed or saddened by what's taking place in the world, why would you want to deprive them of these feelings? Everyone knows that it's only when people feel strongly about something that they'll do something about it. Feeding people pills not only reduces the potency of these feelings, it allows the underlying problems of our society to continue to —"

"I'm going to make us some tea," Claudia said, getting up and moving in the direction of the kitchen.

"Why do you do that?" Phillip asked, sounding slightly annoyed.

"Do what?"

"Try to change the subject."

"I'm not doing it to annoy you. I just really feel like a tea," Claudia said, smiling smugly while walking into the kitchen. "Besides, I'm still listening."

Of course, she knew he wouldn't speak to her about anything serious while she was in the kitchen; he insisted on having face-to-face conversations, a tête-à-tête, as he called them. He required eye contact, body language, a person's aura to embroider the conversation, which was why he despised talking over the phone or using e-mail.

"Would you like one?" she asked him again after a few moments.

"I'll have a camomile, please," he replied. "Warm."

"I know," Claudia said under her breath, remembering how she thought it odd he liked his tea served warm, not hot, that this fact alone was enough to give her mother reason for concern.

"Anything in it?" Claudia asked.

Phillip took his tea one of two ways, depending on his mood. 'As is' normally coincided with a quiet, tranquil frame of mind and involved the tea being served after allowing the tea bag to steep for no more than ten seconds. 'Dressed up' usually indicated a more ostentatious or spirited disposition and involved steeping the tea bag for at least a minute before adding two teaspoons of raw, organic cane sugar and a splash of unpasteurized, organic skim milk. Claudia had her money on 'Dressed up.'

"Dressed up, please," Phillip replied.

Claudia shook her head. Her mother was right. Life with Phillip had become unbearable. Unbearably heavy. The Unbearable Heaviness of Being with Phillip. Claudia smiled. That might make for a good movie, she mused, surveying the assortment of teas on the shelf above the stove. Maybe one of those alternative movies they show at the Westdale Theatre sometimes. I could go and get my camcorder from — oh, quit stalling and get on with it, Claudia, she said to herself, glancing at her watch.

Her mother would be calling in ten minutes, which meant she now had less than ten minutes to tell Phillip she was breaking up with him.

After retrieving the two white porcelain mugs she'd told Phillip she'd bought at a garage sale last month but had really purchased at Pier 1 Imports, she quickly filled them with water, placed them in the microwave and set the timer for two minutes.

When the microwave buzzer went off, she prepared the teas quickly and was about to bring the mugs into the studio when an idea occurred to her. An idea whose time has come, she said to herself, smiling. Setting the two mugs down on the stove, she zipped out into the studio and retrieved her purse, the entire time holding up her finger to Phillip who she knew was itching to resume his diatribe. Upon returning to the kitchen, she withdrew a small vial of Demerol from her purse and dissolved 50 millilitres into his tea along with a bit more cane sugar before bringing it to him.

"As I was saying," Phillip said, as Claudia handed over his mug, "I think that —"

"Oh, hold that thought," Claudia said, interrupting him, starting to walk towards the bathroom. "I'll be back in a minute."

Returning five minutes later, she found Phillip now lying on the floor, curled up in the fetal position, his head resting comfortably on the throw cushion. He looks peaceful, almost benign, Claudia thought as she stepped over him on her way to the front window.

Reaching the window, she began surveying Locke Street, slowly absorbing the mid-afternoon ambience while sipping her Earl Grey tea. A few moments later, the sight of an attractive, middle-aged man stepping out of a Mercedes suspended her visual sweep before being aroused again by the squeals of delight coming from two young, well-dressed women standing arm-in-arm by the bus stop. A minute or so later, after the Locke 7 bus had picked them up and transported them out of sight, Claudia began wondering, as she often had in the past few weeks, who she would end up with, who she was destined —

"They still haven't found them, you know," she heard Phillip say, his words slightly slurred.

"Excuse me?" she said, her eyes once again on the man who had stepped out of the Mercedes.

"The weapons. In Iraq. They still haven't found them."

"Yeah, I know," Claudia replied, solemnly, his words immediately reminding her of the deal they'd made in JFK Airport. Why me? Claudia thought. I mean, even Bush had acknowledged defeat and called off the search. Oh, what the hell am I waiting —

Just then, as her cell phone started ringing (right on time, Mother), Claudia noticed something more than vaguely familiar about the hairstyle of the woman walking along the sidewalk directly beneath their apartment. Oh my God. I don't believe it. It's Maureen.

"Maureen! Maureen!" Claudia started shouting, rapping her hand on the window pane. "Maureen! Up here! Up here!"

To Be Continued . . .

obstacle

Squinting, Maureen Milhaven shielded her eyes against the early afternoon sun in an effort to see who was shouting her name. The sunlight glinting off the windowpane, however, made it temporarily impossible to see anything but a white coffee mug attached to a hand.

"Unbelievable," Maureen said a few moments later, after she'd moved several steps to her right and realized it was Claudia DeAngelo framed in one of the windows above her, waving excitedly.

"Who's that?" Charlotte asked.

"Claudia," Maureen replied, sounding annoyed.

"Oh my God. You mean Claudia 'the-unreciprocated-love-of-your-life' Claudia?" Charlotte said, looking in the direction Maureen had been looking.

"Yes, *that* Claudia. We should get going," Maureen said, motioning for Charlotte to follow her.

"But I want to see her," Charlotte half-whispered. "Which window is it?"

"She's gone," Maureen said, taking hold of Charlotte's arm and starting to pull her along the sidewalk.

"If you think I'm leaving right now, you're crazy," Charlotte said, breaking free of Maureen's grasp. "I've had to listen to you talk about this woman for years. There's no way I'm leaving without getting at least a glimpse of her."

"Fine," Maureen replied, turning and starting to walk away. "You can walk back to the hotel, then."

"You're leaving?"

"Yes," Maureen said, not looking back.

"But what about lunch?" Charlotte called after her, still scanning the windows for Claudia. "It's already after 1:00 p.m. and I'm starving."

"We'll eat somewhere else."

A minute later they were seated inside Maureen's rental car, a navy blue Ford Escort.

"Windows down," Maureen said, simultaneously opening the driver's side window and the sunroof.

"What's wrong with the AC?" Charlotte asked.

"I'm having a cigarette," Maureen replied, pulling a package of Salem Black Label cigarettes from her faux crocodile purse.

"I thought you said those were only in case of an emergency?"

Maureen nodded. "They are. And a Claudia DeAngelo sighting definitely qualifies."

"Oh. Well, are you sure you're allowed to smoke in rental cars?"

"I don't know," Maureen snapped, pulling a cigarette from the package and bringing it to her lips. "Who cares?"

"Okay, relax," Charlotte replied, rolling down the passenger side window. "It was just a question, not an indictment."

"I'm sorry, Char. I just can't believe I saw her, you know?"

"I know, I know. I'd probably be a little freaked out too," Charlotte replied. Then, after watching Maureen try unsuccessfully to light her cigarette several times, she said, "You want me to light that for you?"

"I'm fine," Maureen said, waving her off.

"Yeah, maybe for someone diagnosed with Parkinson's. Look at your hands, Maureen. They're shaking like crazy."

After another four failed attempts, Maureen sighed loudly and passed the lighter to Charlotte, allowing her to light it as she pulled out of her parking spot, beginning to drive north along Locke Street.

"That's where we met," Maureen said a few moments later, pointing her now lit cigarette in the direction of Agnes' Flower Company.

"Who?"

"Claudia."

It was the day before Mother's Day and they were both ordering flowers for their mothers. She'd overheard Claudia telling the owner that the flower shop used to be a home for the men who once worked for the Tuckett Tobacco Company. Minutes later they were strolling down Locke Street and Claudia was giving Maureen her first Hamilton history lesson, telling Maureen who this street was named after, when this building was built, what influences — natural, political, or otherwise — had determined the area's development.

"See this bridge here," Maureen said, gesturing to the train bridge they were now driving over. "It was originally built around 1895, the year the old TH&B — the Toronto-Hamilton-Buffalo — Railway was completed."

"And you're telling me this because . . ." Charlotte asked, giving Maureen a puzzled look.

"Because it was where —"

Maureen stopped herself in mid-sentence, deciding to preserve the memory for herself, the memory of Claudia abruptly grabbing her arm that day and suggesting they hop a train; of the two of them, less than an hour later, laughing and singing and dancing on an empty flatbed car bound for Buffalo; of Claudia shouting that they were like Thelma and Louise, telling Maureen that once the train stopped in Buffalo they were going to rent a convertible and drive all the way to the Grand Canyon; of Maureen silently acknowledging that Claudia was the person she wanted to be with. Forever.

"Never mind," Maureen said, taking a long haul on her cigarette. "It's not important."

What was important, however, was that even back then Maureen knew driving to the Grand Canyon in a convertible with Claudia was more her fantasy, more her utopia, than Claudia's. Which was why she wasn't surprised when, instead of continuing on to Buffalo, Claudia suggested they jump off the train in St. Catharines and buy a couple of bottles of Chardonnay at a liquor store before walking to Lakeside Park, getting drunk, and passing out on a picnic table.

"Oh my God," Charlotte said, suddenly, pinching her nose. "What's that disgusting smell?"

A moment later the pungent odour of fish assaulted Maureen's olfactory senses.

"It's coming from the S&S Supermarket on our right," Maureen replied, pointing her cigarette at the store before making a left on Jackson Street. "It's an Asian Fish Market. It used be a Calabria grocery store."

Charlotte chuckled. "You sound like my personal tour guide."

"What? Oh. Really? You think so?" Maureen said, smiling, colliding with another memory.

It was what she used to call Claudia. Each time they went for a walk or a drive around Hamilton, Claudia would bathe her in trivia, facts, and folklore about the city, her historical commentary oftentimes making an entirely different city appear before Maureen's eyes, enabling her to imagine what it used to be like to live in a particular area ten, twenty-five, fifty, one hundred, even one hundred and fifty years prior — the streets changing names or disappearing completely; businesses and buildings evaporating or being erected; the people themselves transforming, their fashions, hairstyles, and ideas altering to suit the times.

"Did you know," Maureen said, suddenly finding it difficult to contain her excitement, "that the street we're on right now — Jackson Street — was named after the guy who helped create a liberal arts college for women in Hamilton almost one hundred and fifty years ago?"

"Really?" Charlotte replied, sounding mildly intrigued, before adding, "Well, did *you* know that this street is also a dead end?"

"Oh piss, you're right," Maureen said, slowly applying the brakes. "What the hell was I thinking?"

"Judging by your expression, I would say you were making a detour down memory lane."

"Very funny," Maureen replied, her eyes now drifting through Jackson Park, reflexively gravitating to the spot where she and Claudia used to sit and read and tan, smiling to herself when she saw the slide platform, recalling the time she and Claudia used it to give an abridged performance of *Romeo & Juliet* to a construction crew taking their lunch break in the small park.

"So, was I right?" Charlotte asked, once Maureen had turned the car around.

"About what?"

"The detour you just made."

Maureen smiled. "Maybe," she said, turning left onto Poulette Street and looking at her hair in the rear-view mirror. She'd had it cut a few days ago in the same style she'd had before she'd left Hamilton — the way Claudia had liked it.

"You're still taking it, aren't you?"

"Maybe."

"Care to share what's going through that brain of yours right now?"

"It's not that thrilling."

"Try me."

Maureen hesitated, then said, "I was just thinking about what Claudia used to say about certain books."

Charlotte waited a few moments for Maureen to continue and, when she didn't, said, "Well? What did she used to say?"

"Oh, right. Sorry. She used to say she wasn't fond of books with too much character development. She said she was more interested in sampling slices of people's lives. She preferred to have a few details and then let her imagination fill in the rest."

"Oh my God, really? That's exactly how *I* feel," Charlotte replied. "Give me a sprinkling of setting, a dash of character development, a pinch of plot, and little snippets of dialogue, and that's enough. That's what gets me going. I like stories that leave me hanging, where the writer merely gives me a sneak peek into what's going on and then relies on me and *my* imagination to decide what's going to happen next, what the rest of the scene or story will —"

It was at this point that Maureen stopped listening to Charlotte and, while waiting for a break in traffic on Main Street, once again slipped into reverie, sifting through snapshots of the times she and

Claudia had spent together, constructing a mental photo gallery of their relationship.

"I can't believe I just ran into Claudia DeAngelo!" Maureen shouted, a few moments later, interrupting Charlotte.

"Did you ever tell her how you felt?" Charlotte asked.

"Only about a million times. In my head."

"Why only in your head?"

"I don't know. I guess I just couldn't bear to have her say she didn't feel the same way. I mean, have you ever wanted something so bad you were terrified of it not working out?"

Charlotte nodded. "Sure. All the time."

"Claudia was everything I'd ever dreamed of. She had looks, intelligence, a good job, a killer body, a great family. Everything."

"It seems to me you're forgetting one very important detail here, Moe."

"What's that?"

"She wasn't gay."

Maureen sighed, nodding her head. "I know."

"Well, that's a fairly serious obstacle to a successful lesbian relationship."

"Ahh," Maureen growled. "Why am I doing this to myself?"

"Because you're human."

Maureen shook her head. "You know, thinking back on it now, I can't believe her reaction when I told her I was moving to Vancouver. You know what she did? She got all excited and told me she always wanted a friend on the west coast and that now she'd be able to come out and visit me and the two of us could go skiing in Whistler. Do you believe that? I mean, how could she not know how I felt? How could she not realize that the only reason I was moving to Vancouver was because I couldn't bear to spend another minute with her without being *with* her?"

"Because *she's* human."

"What a bitch!" Maureen shouted, suddenly stomping on the accelerator and making a quick right turn onto Main Street, cutting in front of a GO Transit bus, prompting the driver of the bus to blast his horn three times. "I can't believe she actually called out to me. And *waved* to me. I mean, what the hell was she thinking?"

"I really have no idea," Charlotte replied, nervously, glancing back at the GO bus now riding the Escort's rear bumper. "But maybe we should pull over somewhere and talk about this. Maybe driving isn't the —"

"I'm fine. Really, I am."

"Honestly?"

Maureen nodded. "I could probably do with a topic change, though."

"Well, in that case, what's with all the billboards in this city?"

"What do you mean?"

"Haven't you noticed? It's like there's an anti-advertising campaign or something going on here."

"Really?" Maureen replied, looking at the signage in an effort to see what Charlotte was talking about. "I guess I've been a little preoccupied."

"I believe 'obsessed' is the correct term."

Maureen chuckled. "Look at me, Char," she said, shaking her head. "I'm smoking. I mean, how pathetic am I? Wait, don't answer that."

The two women smiled at each other, then broke out laughing. A few moments later, Maureen gave her cigarette a disparaging look and flicked it out the sunroof.

"Good riddance!" she shouted.

"By the way," Charlotte said, noticing another tarnished billboard, this one with a giant black 'X' painted over a car advertisement. "Where are we going?"

"I don't know," Maureen replied. "I'm just driving."

"Well, what do you feel like doing?"

Maureen shrugged. "Want to get out of the city?"

"Sure."

"For the afternoon or the rest of the day?"

"Your choice."

"Well, if we go for the rest of the day, I'd like to stop off at the hotel and get changed."

"Me too."

"So, then, which do you want?"

"Red light."

"What?"

"Red light! Red light!" Charlotte screamed, pointing at the red light at Queen Street.

"Oh, piss!" Maureen shouted, bringing the Escort to a skidding stop just in time to receive an irate glare from a pregnant woman walking her dog across the intersection.

"Sorry," Maureen said, hanging her head out the car window.

"Jesus. That was close," Charlotte said, breathing a huge sigh of relief.

"I know, I know. I'm a complete mess. All I keep thinking about is Claudia."

"Listen, why don't you go back and talk to her?"

"What? Are you serious?"

"Why not? I mean, it's certainly healthier than endlessly obsessing about her. Not to mention a lot safer — especially while you're behind the wheel of a car."

"But you said it yourself, she's not gay."

"I said she *wasn't* gay. Who knows, maybe now she is."

"What?"

"Hey, stranger things have happened. I mean, not all of us wake up one morning when we're seven and realize we're lesbian. Sometimes it takes a while for some women to realize it. Maybe she's been through enough loser guys by now that she's ready to try something different."

"Wait. Are you suggesting that I —"

"Excuse me."

Maureen turned her head in the direction of the voice and saw a man seated on a blue and white full-suspension Giant mountain bike tossing a lit cigarette butt at her.

"The world is not your personal ashtray," the man said before pedalling through the intersection.

. . . . **To Be Continued . . .**

that's positive, right?

"Nice shot," Stephanie said, pulling up alongside Shaun.

"Thanks," Shaun replied, smiling.

"I think her hair might be on fire."

"Seriously?"

Stephanie nodded. "Too much hair product."

"We should probably get the hell out of here then," Shaun said, turning left on Hess Street and beginning to pedal faster, the mountain bike lurching forward in response to his increased pace.

He'd bought the bike last summer — the day after turning thirty-seven — from Main Cycle in East Hamilton and was instantly hooked, spending hours riding the dozens of trails around Hamilton, Dundas, Ancaster, and Waterdown. Kristan, his wife of ten years, chided him, saying he was having a pre-middle-aged crisis and was trying to get back in touch with his youth, but the truth was, ever since suffering his third concussion in two years while playing lacrosse, he'd been looking for something to replace it.

"Where are we going?" he heard Stephanie call after him.

"You'll see," Shaun replied.

Five minutes later they were taking off their helmets, their bikes now parked near the small snack shack at Bayfront Park, joking about the woman's hair going up in flames, that she looked like Kramer in that episode of *Seinfeld* or Michael Jackson during that Pepsi commercial.

"So what's this place called again?" Stephanie asked, retrieving her bottle of orange-flavoured Gatorade from her bicycle.

"Bayfront Park," Shaun replied.

"I never even knew this was here," Stephanie said, surveying the park, quickly taking in the boat launch; the gazebo; the clumps of people picnicking on the grass; the dozens and dozens of people walking, running, biking, and inline skating along the waterfront path. "It's really nice."

Shaun nodded his head in agreement. "They're probably going to expand the path right through to Toronto — connect Hamilton with Burlington, Oakville, Mississauga, and Toronto."

"That's a great idea."

"Yeah, I hope they do it," Shaun said, briefly regarding the engagement ring on Stephanie's left hand before casting his gaze out over Lake Ontario, his eyes rustling into the various nooks and crannies along the distant shoreline where he and his mother, a widow now for nearly thirty years, used to take him out in the family canoe, paddling around, teaching him about the surrounding ecosystem.

"The Iroquois used to refer to this place as 'Macassah,'" he said, recalling his mother's words. "It means, 'beautiful waters.'"

"Wow . . ." Stephanie said, looking down at the water, adding, a few moments later, "Well, times have certainly changed, haven't they?"

Shaun chuckled, nodding his head. The water was now a yellow-brown colour, like run-off from a manure pile during a heavy rain. The first time he and his mother went out he thought the people fishing along the shore were idiots for being there, for believing that fish would breathe this stuff. They did, though. Within minutes he saw them, bobbing to the surface beside their canoe, performing lethargic rolls, their eyes vacant, their bellies bloated and blistered like kids in a UNICEF commercial; others came charging out of the water, writhing and contorting as though trying to wrench themselves free of their contaminated skins, while some rammed themselves head first against the aluminium hull of the canoe, their palsied thuds echoing in his knees, ricocheting up his spine. It was the first time he had come face to face with the harmful effects associated with factory effluent.

"They're starting to clean it up, though," Shaun said. "The water, the harbour, Cootes Paradise — the whole area."

"Wasn't your mother involved in that?" Stephanie asked, retrieving a PowerBar from the micro seat-pack beneath her bicycle seat.

Shaun nodded. "She and a lot of other people lobbied the government for years to return this area to its original —"

"Are those swans over there?" Stephanie asked, interrupting him, her hand pointing west.

"Yep," Shaun said. "There are all kinds of birds down here — swans, Canada geese, blue herons, hawks, eagles, ducks, kingfishers."

"Impressive. Drink?" Stephanie said, offering him her Gatorade.

"No thanks," Shaun replied. "I'm okay."

"PowerBar?"

"Naw, I'm not really hungry."

"You sure? I've got two."

"Naw, I'm fine. Thanks, though."

"No problem," Stephanie said, starting to unwrap the PowerBar after taking another swig of her Gatorade.

"You know," Shaun said, giving her Trek mountain bike a once over. "I've been meaning to ask you where you got your bike."

"At Main Cycle."

"Hey, that's where I got my bike."

"I know. You were the one who told me to go there. Remember?"

"Oh, yeah. Right. It must've slipped my mind."

Stephanie shook her head and smiled. After taking a seat on a nearby bench she patted the empty space beside her to indicate she wanted Shaun to sit down beside her.

"Okay, Shaun," she said once he was seated, "not that I don't find what we've been talking about interesting, but I'm fairly certain you didn't invite me out just so we could talk about birds and bicycles. Am I right?"

Shaun nodded his head slowly. Stephanie was right. There was more. A lot more. But, setting aside the fact that he and Stephanie hadn't always gotten along, Shaun didn't like the idea that what he really wanted to talk about might seem as though he was taking advantage of the fact that Stephanie was a marriage counsellor. It was how he felt whenever people immediately asked him for the latest stock market tip when they found out he was an investment broker.

"Hello. Earth to Shaun," Stephanie said, waving the now partially unwrapped PowerBar in front of his face.

Shaun blinked. "Have you noticed anything different about Kristan?"

"I don't know, should I?"

"I was just wondering if you'd noticed, well . . . anything, you know, out of the . . . well, the truth is, we haven't had sex in a while."

Shaun couldn't believe he'd said it. Actually, strike that. He couldn't believe he'd *had* to say it. Until three months ago, he and Kristan had sex all the time, as often as five times a day. It wasn't unusual for them to spend an entire day in bed. They'd pretend it was their private island or their sex raft or their —

"Exactly how long is 'a while'?" Stephanie asked before taking a tiny bite of her PowerBar.

"Months. Three, actually."

"Is that a change for you guys?"

"If I thought it was typical, do you think I'd be talking to you about this?" Shaun replied.

Stephanie smiled. "Trust me, Shaun," she said, her tone soothing, comforting. "I realize this is difficult. The reason I asked was I know plenty of couples in their late thirties who don't have sex on a regular basis."

"So you're suggesting this is normal?"

"Hmmm," Stephanie said, bring the PowerBar to her lips. "I don't really like to use the term, 'normal.' It's too ambiguous."

"Well, then, in your experience?"

"In my experience, there are plenty of examples of couples who go through phases where they don't have sex for extended periods of time."

Shaun pondered this information for a while. The longest he and Kristan had gone without having sex until three months ago was four days — which was the long weekend she'd gone to Ottawa for a lawyer's conference.

"Do you think she's having an affair?"

Stephanie coughed, held up her finger for Shaun to wait a second, and then, once she'd swallowed the small piece of PowerBar that had been in her mouth, said, "Why are you asking me?"

"Because you're her sister. I figured she might have told you."

"Well, she hasn't said anything to me."

"Would you tell me if she had?"

Stephanie paused for a second, then shook her head. "No. But I probably wouldn't deny it either."

"I see," Shaun said, rubbing the stubble on his chin. He was trying to grow a goatee, like the one Stephanie's fiancé, Jacobus, had. He wondered if Stephanie had noticed. "By the way, how are you and Jacobus getting along?"

"About as well as we were thirty minutes ago when you asked me that same question."

"So, no problems then?"

"None that I can think of."

"And your sex life, it's . . . it's okay?"

"Excuse me?" Stephanie said, giving Shaun a surprised look.

"Oh come on, Steph. I just told you about me and Kristan. I'm not asking for details or how often . . . well maybe, ah, forget it. I'm sorry. I'm just a little . . ."

Stephanie smiled. "If it'll make you feel better, Jacobus and I are doing just fine in that department."

"Really? That's good. That's . . . great," Shaun said, trying to sound sincere, wondering how big a jackass Stephanie thought he was for asking her these sorts of personal questions.

Leaning forward, he caught a glimpse of a great blue heron lifting off from the edge of the water near the far point. "Hey, look, there's a —" he started to say, then, leaning back, his eyes still on the heron, he asked, "So, would you say that you and Jacobus have an open relationship?"

Stephanie chuckled. "I'm not sure what you mean by 'open.'"

"Well, are the two of you in a monogamous relationship or have you agreed that dating other people is, you know, alright?"

"Once again, Shaun, not that it's any of your business, but we're monogamous."

Shaun nodded. "I thought so."

Smiling, Stephanie set her Gatorade bottle down beside her, crossed her legs, and said, "Okay, do all these questions about my relationship with Jacobus have a point?"

Shaun delayed his response until the couple walking past their bench were out of earshot and then shrugged and said, "I read somewhere that if your partner isn't interested in having sex, it's usually a sign she's having sex with someone else."

Stephanie giggled.

"What? That's not true?"

"Not always," Stephanie replied. "In fact, not even usually. Usually there's some other reason responsible for the lack of sexual intimacy in a relationship. It annoys me that people always assume the reason is because the person is cheating."

"Even if the person calls out another man's name when she's sleeping?"

Stephanie, about to take a bite of her PowerBar, withdrew the bar from her mouth. "Is that what Kristan's doing?"

Shaun nodded.

"Lots of people do that," Stephanie said, after a moment.

"Name one," Shaun replied, unconvinced.

"It used to happen to one of my roommates all the time," Stephanie said, brushing a phantom piece of lint off her nylon cycling shirt. "She used to call out the names of her old boyfriends almost every night."

"Really?" Shaun said, thinking for the first time that Stephanie knew more about Kristan than she was letting on.

Stephanie nodded. "On Sundays and Tuesdays, it was William. On Mondays and Wednesdays, David. And on Thursdays and Saturdays, Andrew."

"What about Fridays?"

"Nothing. Absolutely nothing."

"Her day of rest, I suppose," Shaun said, duly impressed by Stephanie's imaginative powers, yet giving her a look as though he thought she was full of shit.

"I'm not making this up, Shaun," Stephanie insisted. "I used to invite people over just to listen to her. It was a complete riot."

"I'm sure it was," Shaun replied. "And, out of consideration for you meeting with me today, I'll agree to temporarily suspend my scepticism and believe this story of yours. However, did your roommate ever have," and then, leaning in close to Stephanie, he whispered the rest of the question in her ear.

"Kristan's having orgasms in her sleep?"

"Jesus, Stephanie. Tell the whole world, why don't you?" Shaun said, swiftly scanning the immediate area to see if anyone had overheard.

"Sorry," Stephanie said, clasping her hand over her mouth.

"It's okay. I don't think anyone heard you. And yes, Kristan's having orgasms in her sleep."

"Are you sure?"

"Positive."

"How do you know?"

"Because I've seen my wife having an orgasm before."

"Well, okay. But, how do you *know*-know?"

Shaun paused, waiting until an elderly couple had shuffled a little further along the walkway before continuing to speak.

"The first time I saw her was almost three months ago. I was up late, reading a *Maclean's* magazine when I heard all this noise and commotion coming from our bedroom and when I entered the room it was like *The Exorcist* meets *When Harry Met Sally* — only instead of moaning like some crazed woman and shouting 'Fuck me! Fuck me!' while screwing a crucifix she was moaning and humping our body pillow while screaming some guy's name."

Stephanie paused in mid-chew, tilting her head slightly up and to the right, making Shaun wonder if she was now imagining Kristan writhing around on their king-sized Alexandria bed with three-hundred–thread count sheets, her bare, cream-coloured legs curled around the body pillow, the arches of her feet sliding up and down the pillow, the —

"So, what do you think I should do?"

"About what?"

"About this whole situation."

"Right. Well, um, how many times has it happened?"

"Seven."

"In the last three months? "

Shaun shook his head. "In the last month."

"You mean you've actually witnessed her doing this seven times in the past month?"

Shaun nodded. "And I don't know what to do about it. I mean, am I supposed to just go up to her and say, 'So, honey, I've been noticing lately that you're having orgasms in your sleep while screaming some guy's name'?"

"That's one approach," Stephanie said, starting to laugh before abruptly stopping and taking hold of Shaun's arm. "Hey, are you okay?"

"It's nothing," he replied, gently pulling away from her. He could feel his throat tightening, his lips starting to quiver, making it difficult to speak. "I'm sorry."

"Shaun, what's wrong?" Stephanie said, returning her hand to his arm. "There's something more going on, isn't there?"

Shaun hesitated, then nodded his head. "This morning, while I was shaving, I thought there was something really odd about the way Kristan was acting. I mean, she's normally very composed, very unemotional, very — well, you know how she is, you're her sister. But this morning she was not at all herself. She was completely frazzled. In fact, I think she'd been crying but when I asked her what was wrong, she told me she had to go and ran out of the house. After she left, I found something in the bathroom. In the garbage, actually . . ."

Shaun stopped speaking.

"Go on," Stephanie gently urged. "It's okay."

"It was a pregnancy test. One of those litmus stick things. It was blue. That's positive, right?"

Stephanie didn't respond.

"I thought so. I can't believe this," Shaun said, shaking his head. "I've been wanting to have a baby with her for God knows how long and now, not only do I have to listen to her screaming some other guy's name while she humps our body pillow, I find out she's pregnant."

"Who's the guy?"

"Huh?"

"The guy. You said she screams out his name. Do you know him?"

"Well, that's where things really get interesting because it's someone we both —"

"Shhhh!"

"Excuse me?"

"I'm sorry, Shaun. But could you just hang on for a second?" Stephanie said, putting up her hand and turning her head in the direction of the parking lot.

"What is it?" Shaun asked, completely taken aback that Stephanie had just cut him off.

"Just one second. Please."

"What's going on?" Shaun whispered.

"That music. It's coming from someone's car. Can you hear it?"

Shaun listened for a few seconds, thought he may have heard something but couldn't be certain. "No."

"It sounds like this jazz tune that's been stuck in my head since last Saturday."

"I can't even hear —"

"Please, Shaun. Trust me, I don't mean to be rude and I feel like such a horrible person right now for not giving you my full attention, but I've been trying to find out who plays this tune ever since I heard it. It's driving me completely mad. Are you sure you can't hear it? It sounds like . . . oh, oh, wait, it's on the tip of my tongue. It's Winters. No, Winston. No, no, ahh, I know, I know, it's, it's —"

. . . . To Be Continued . . .

interloper

"Wynton Marsalis," Randy said under his breath, walking quickly by the woman without looking at her.

When he reached his blue Ford F-150 pickup truck, Randy made a concerted effort not to let his gaze pass over the area where the woman was, wanting to preserve the sound of her voice without an accompanying physical description.

It was something he started doing years ago, when he lived in Toronto. During his lunch hour, he'd hop on a streetcar or the subway or sit in Nathan Phillips Square or on a bench in the Eaton Centre and, while listening to the medley of conversations, mentally embroider the voices with personalities, physical characteristics, careers, backgrounds, and lifestyles, taking bits of overheard dialogue and piecing together a semi-continuous narrative, creating a compelling collection of short stories.

While driving out of the parking lot at Bayfront Park, he imagined this woman to be in her late-twenties, brunette, 5'6", perhaps 5'7" tall, 125 pounds, and if not physically fit, then at least physically active. She's a telemarketer, Randy said to himself, or someone who works in sales, perhaps in the serving industry. That's it, she's a waitress. No, a bartender. A bartender who works at Rankin's Bar & Grill in East Hamilton, works out at Body One Fitness in Dundas, enjoys inline skating, afternoon walks, and wearing sexy lingerie.

By the time he was driving east on Strachan Street, Randy had decided on her attire for the evening — a white cotton halter-top and pleated cotton skirt with leather cascade wedges — and had placed himself in the scene, striding confidently up to the bar, wearing his recently acquired Hugo Boss suit.

"Hi there, I'm Randy," he'd say, giving her a wink while casually mounting the bar stool at Rankin's.

"So, Randy, what's your line?" she'd reply, sounding as though she were already bored with him.

"My line?" he'd say, giving her a quizzical look.

"Yeah, every guy's got one."

At this point he would give her a look as though he were deciding whether or not she was worthy of his line, and then, after a moment or two, he'd say, "I despise predictability, especially in people. Being predictable is one of the worst things a person can be."

She would smile and he would go on to tell her that he enjoyed people who were full of contradictions and surprises, who were rarely, if ever, consistent in their actions; people who continually defied characterisation, who were always evolving, changing, transforming themselves into some new creation, whose behaviour remained beyond the latest definitions provided by talk show psychologists. "These are the kind of people who fascinate me," he would conclude.

"Wow," she would say, obviously impressed. "I have to admit, that's one line I've never heard before."

For the next while they would continue to make the requisite small talk and she would continue to find him charming, humorous, intelligent, and informative. At some point in the conversation he would subtly steer the topic around to music and she would eventually ask him what kind of music he liked.

"Here, have a quick listen," he'd say, pulling out his Sony walkman and holding the ear piece close to her ear before pushing PLAY.

"Oh my God. That's him," she would say.

"Who?"

"That guy."

"You mean Wynton Marsalis?"

"Ya. I've been trying to figure out that guy's name for days."

"You like him?"

She would nod, then tell him she was just starting to appreciate jazz, that as she got older she'd noticed her musical tastes were changing. He would nod and tell her that this was normal.

"Unless, of course, you had a grandfather who loved jazz and then you learned to appreciate it before you could talk."

"And you did?"

He would nod. "My grandfather was crazy about jazz."

"Did he play anything?"

"The saxophone."

"And what about his grandson?"

"The sax, the trumpet, *and* the piano."

"Really?" she'd reply, excitedly. "You can play all three?"

After he nodded, she would start to look at him differently, as though he wasn't just some stupid shmuck who went around hitting on female bartenders.

"I can't believe you were listening to Wynton Marsalis," she'd say, smiling warmly. "Talk about coincidences."

At her request, he would pick her up the following evening at her house, accepting her invitation to have dinner at Las Aguas as well as a few drinks afterwards in Hess Village before she accepted his invitation to visit his apartment, to having another couple of drinks and then retiring to his bedroom.

When he saw her taking off her clothes, exposing her matching black mesh bustier and panties, he pushed PAUSE on his creation, intent on saving the rest of the scene for later, for when he was in his recently acquired king-sized orthopedic pillow-top mattress and box spring.

"Speaking of being put on pause," Randy said, aloud, turning right on James Street, heading in the direction of downtown. "I suppose I should tell Juanita I've met someone else."

He was certain she'd understand. He'd told her when they met — three weeks ago at Different Drummer bookstore in Burlington — that he wasn't interested in traditional relationships. Of course, Juanita would still be upset.

"What do you mean you've met someone else?" she'd undoubtedly shout at him, her perfect nostrils flaring, her right foot alternately tapping and clawing the floor like a bull ready to charge. "Who is she?"

"Juanita, relax. I told you before. I can't help it. It's just the way I am. I don't like to be tied down."

Once he had mentally worked things out with Juanita, Randy turned on his radio, punching the first pre-set button, 91.1, and immediately recognizing Dizzy Gillespie's trumpet blaring through the truck's speaker system. After fine tuning the sound, Randy began humming and snapping his fingers to the swinging beat and a few moments later the interior of his truck had suddenly morphed into a smoke-filled, backstreet jazz bar where he and his grandfather and Dizzy were now on stage together, working their instruments into a frenzy, the audience held breathless, completely spellbound by the trio.

That sure is some sweet stuff, Randy said to himself as he drove past Luina Station — Hamilton's old train depot — thinking of the numerous times he'd listened to his grandfather telling him what it was like to hear guys like Dizzy, Duke Ellington, Fats Waller, and Count Basie perform at The Flamingo Club in Hamilton during the 1930s and 1940s.

"Let 'er rip, Diz!" Randy shouted after he and his grandfather pulled their instruments away from their lips.

Leaning back in his chair, his eyes alternating between his grandfather, Dizzy, and the audience, Randy felt a surge of euphoria rushing through him, causing his skin to tingle, making him feel as though he could —

"What the hell is that?" Randy said, aloud.

Even before he noticed the audience members starting to turn around or get up from their seats in an effort to determine where the noise was coming from, Randy heard the sound of a way, *way* too-loud synthesized bass drum intruding on Dizzy's solo.

Setting aside his saxophone, Randy checked his side-view mirror and immediately located the interloper; a souped-up car approaching on his left. By the time the car pulled up alongside his truck at the

York Street traffic light, the sound of the bass being ejected from its open windows and sunroof had completely pulverized the sound of Dizzy's trumpet, prompting Randy to increase the volume on his stereo until Dizzy once again reigned supreme.

Smiling, Randy was about to pick up his saxophone and re-join Dizzy when he heard a horn honking. Looking out the driver's side window he saw a young guy, probably no more than twenty-five, wearing short, dyed blonde hair, sunglasses, a white tank top, and a barbed wire tattoo on his right shoulder waving at him through the sunroof of his car. His companion, a much younger Asian girl dressed in a beige jogging suit and '70s-style sunglasses seemed oblivious to everything and was busy adjusting her bra in the passenger seat.

The guy honked his horn again, this time shouting something at Randy that Randy couldn't make out, so he hit the POWER button on his stereo.

The young guy's music was now off.

"Hey man, that's Dizzy Gillespie — right?" the young guy hollered, sticking his head out the sunroof.

Randy looked at the young guy and nodded slowly, slightly surprised.

"I thought so," the young guy said, smiling. "That cat was one serious trumpet technician, huh? You ever get a chance to see him in concert?"

Randy shook his head and started rolling up his window.

. . . . **To Be Continued . . .**

wannabe

"Yeah, well, it was nice talking to you, too, Mr. Music Horder," Devin said, watching the man in the blue truck rolling up his window.

A second later, when the light changed to green, Devin stomped on the accelerator, the yellow Volkswagen's 115bhp 1.9-litre TDI engine roaring to life, the Uniroyal Rallye tires screeching momentarily before biting into the hot asphalt, causing the Volkswagen to lurch forward, accelerating quickly. After slamming it into second gear, Devin waved at the guy in the blue truck through the Volkswagen's sunroof before laughing out loud and reaching over and grabbing his girlfriend's right breast, giving it a playful squeeze.

"Damn, Lili," he said, immediately removing his hand from her breast, as though he'd just come in contact with something extremely toxic. "I told you I like the real thing."

"This *is* the real thing," Lili insisted.

Devin reached over and squeezed her gel-padded bra. "No, *that*, is 100% gel. I know the difference. Trust me."

"So what if it is? What's the big deal?"

"What's the big . . . what's the big . . . I'll *tell* you what the big . . ."

Devin inhaled loudly, shoving the air deep inside his lungs and holding it there for a count of five before letting it out slowly, evenly, attempting to disperse the anger swelling inside him.

Devin's sister had started out this way, putting on a false display, wearing bras and pants and shirts and make-up that accentuated or enhanced or hid what she had; until she took them off and revealed what she really had — often to the disappointment of her numerous partners — prompting her to begin modifying her body with breast implants, collagen lip injections, liposuction, coloured contacts, and Botox, all before the age of twenty-eight. And then, the year she turned thirty, more modifications were necessary: a double mastectomy from breast cancer, medication and twice-weekly therapy sessions to treat her depression, as well as stitches and plastic surgery to cover the scars from two attempted suicides.

"Well?" Lili said impatiently.

"Well what?" Devin snapped, downshifting and braking for the light at King Street.

"Are you going to finish your sentence?"

Devin sighed, gazing indifferently at the scenery outside the car while gathering his thoughts, his eyes dipping into Gore Park, hopping from the large fountain to the statue of Queen Victoria to the two middle-aged men seated on a bench feeding some pigeons.

"Why do you think you need to —" he started to say, then, noticing that Lili had suddenly scrunched down in her seat, he asked. "What are you doing?"

"Hiding."

"From who?"

"That woman," Lili said pointing her finger out the front window.

Devin looked in the direction of Lili's finger and counted at least half a dozen women mixed in with several men and a handful of kids now crossing the street in front of his car.

"Which one?" he asked.

"The old one. The one wearing the yellow cardigan and lime green polyester pants."

"Who is she?" Devin asked, watching the elderly woman shuffling across the street.

"Her name's Agnes. She used to volunteer at the hospital where my mom works until they got rid of her because she was always talking to herself and forgetting what she was supposed to be doing."

"Why are you hiding from her?"

"Because if she sees me she'll insist we pull over and talk to her for hours."

When the delayed right turn traffic light came on, Devin waited for a few jaywalkers to get through the intersection, then made a quick right onto King Street, immediately accelerating past a Ford Windstar and slicing in front of it before snaking around a Chevy Cavalier.

After running a red light in front of The Hamilton Art Gallery, he turned to Lili and said, "Okay, back to what I was saying, why do you think you need to wear something like that?" pointing at her bra.

Lili, now fully upright in her seat, glanced down at her bra. "Because my breasts are too small."

"What?" said Devin, looking at her in disbelief. "You're joking, right?"

Lili shook her head.

"Lili, you have *perfect* breasts. You're a 34 C."

"I want to get implants."

"Implants! Those are like the worst things you can get."

"They're a lot safer now."

"I'm not talking about safety. I'm talking about —"

"Watch out," Lili said, pointing at the car in front of them.

A moment before Lili's warning, Devin had noticed the rusted green Neon switching lanes, had checked his blind spot, and downshifted to second gear. After letting out the clutch, he switched lanes, sped passed the Neon, then momentarily considered accelerating and running the yellow light at Queen Street before reconsidering and applying the brakes.

"Listen, Lili," he said while coming to a controlled stop at the light, "I'm not talking about safety. I'm talking about the fact that you were born with this," he said, pointing at her breasts. "This is you. You should be happy with what you have and not want to add things to it."

Lili adjusted her bra. "You add things to your car all the time."

"A car is different. It's not . . . it's not . . . living! Messing with your body is like messing with nature. It's not natural."

"We should have dinner here again," Lili said, pointing out the passenger side window at La Luna restaurant. "I really liked their —"

"Lili," Devin said, his right hand now tightly gripping the stick shift, his left foot jamming the clutch pedal hard into the floorboard. "I'm serious. You have beautiful breasts. Why would you want to hack them up and pervert your body with implants? I mean, it's bad enough you wear these things," he said, taking his hand off the stick shift and once again squeezing her bra.

"Stop it, Devin. People are watching."

"Who? Where?"

Lili pointed in the direction of two people — a man and a woman — standing at the bus stop outside La Luna restaurant. Both of them were gawking at the position of Devin's right hand.

Still squeezing the bra, Devin leaned to his right. "What the hell are you looking at?" he said, frowning at the two onlookers.

The man and the woman exchanged looks, shook their heads, and half-laughed before the man, after repositioning his grey fedora, responded to Devin's question by saying, "You mean aside from another Eminem wannabe in a souped-up, repainted Honda Civic?"

This time it was Devin who half-laughed, shook his head and, with his hand still on Lili's bra, said, "Listen up, you circa 1955 *Casablanca*-looking idiot, not that it's any of your business, but a) Eminem sucks, b) I wouldn't wanna be anyone *but* me, and c) this ain't no souped-up, repainted Honda Civic, which, if *you* weren't some ignorant, fedora-wearing, Humphrey Bogart–wannabe, you would've already known."

Then, just as the Bogart-wannabe opened his mouth to say something, Devin simultaneously applied the brakes and the accelerator, causing the Volkswagen's tires to spin and screech and spew white, rubber-scented smoke into the air.

. . . . **To Be Continued . . .**

what's there to know?

"I don't think he liked your hat," Sadie said, watching the Volkswagen peel away.

"Yeah, and I think he took *The Fast and the Furious* just a little too seriously," Guy replied, taking off his fedora and fanning the air around his face.

"Well, he's right about one thing, though," Sadie said.

"What, that Eminem sucks?" Guy said, putting his fedora back on.

"No. I happen to like Eminem, so in my opinion, he's wrong about that. What he's right about is that the car he's driving ain't no souped-up, repainted Honda Civic. And that's because he's driving an Mk4 Volkswagen Golf with a JBS turbo charger."

Guy whistled. "Well check out Ms. *Car and Driver* over here."

"Just one of the many things you can find out from reading what other people leave behind on our public transportation system," Sadie replied, reaching into her canvas tote bag and pulling out a car magazine.

"You found this on the bus?" Guy said, taking the magazine from Sadie.

Sadie nodded. "The article starts on page 41. The guy is from Hamilton. He bought a stock Volkswagen Golf Mk4 two years ago and started remodelling it, adding things like a front spoiler, racing seats, Audi door handles, CD player, hydraulic suspension system — and the JBS turbo. Every few months he adds something else to it."

"Wow," Guy said, giving Sadie a 'I never thought I'd hear you talking about cars like this' expression. "I never thought I'd hear you talking about cars like this."

"Well, I didn't say I liked them. I just wanted you to know it wasn't a Honda Civic he was driving."

"Look at this magazine," Guy said, gawking at a photograph on page 37. "It's nothing more than soft porn."

"Yeah, I know," replied Sadie, nodding. "It reminds me of those old biker magazines my uncle used to have in his garage, the ones with all the topless biker babes straddling Harleys. Only these women are a lot younger — and they're wearing designer clothes."

"Do women really get off on this kind of thing?" Guy asked, pointing to the photograph of two young women in micro-shorts draped over the hood of a Volkswagen, their oversized, augmented breasts spilling out of their halter-tops.

Sadie shook her head, her long blonde curls swooshing over her shoulder blades. "Not in my case. Ever since I saw *Risky Business*, public transportation is what does it for me."

Guy smiled. He'd met Sadie a while ago, at an Earth First! meeting. She grew up playing and hiking in the Red Hill Creek area and knew firsthand the devastating effects that personal vehicles and expressways could have on the natural environment.

"So," Guy said, closing the magazine and handing it back to Sadie, "are you telling me you've done it on a train before?"

Sadie smiled mischievously. "Trains, planes, buses, streetcars, subways."

"Really?"

"You know the old saying, once you go public transportation, you never go back."

Guy smiled. "Sadie, my darling, to quote Greg Kinnear in *As Good As It Gets*, you overwhelm me."

"What can I say, I get off on helping the environment."

"Apparently, you also get off *while* helping the environment."

Sadie giggled, her head falling forward, immediately pursued by an avalanche of hair.

"Well, lady," Guy said, standing up and tugging on the brim of his hat, "as much as I hate to leave this discussion, I have to get *on* this bus," nodding in the direction of the approaching West Hamilton 5C bus.

"You're positive you don't want to come with me to Montreal next weekend?" Sadie asked.

"I think I'm going to have to pass."

"You sure? I'm taking public transit," she said, giving him a more than slightly suggestive smile.

Guy laughed, "Well, now that I know about your fetish, I may reconsider."

"Give me a call if you change your mind."

"Will do," he said, bending over and air-kissing her cheek. "I'll see ya later, Sadie. And thanks for the info."

"My pleasure," he heard her shout after him as he boarded the bus.

"Tant pis pour moi," Guy said, waving at Sadie through the bus window.

"What's too bad for you?" the bus driver said.

"Oh, nothing," Guy replied, showing the driver his pass. "Just talking to myself."

"Well, as long as you don't start swearing, I'm sure the rest of them won't mind too much," the driver said with a smile, gesturing to the other passengers.

After placing his transit pass back in his wallet, Guy began walking towards the back of the bus, nodding at the two elderly gentlemen holding carved wooden canes seated near the front and smiling at the young pregnant woman seated on one of the benches before nearly careening into an elderly woman wearing a yellow cardigan and lime green polyester pants when the bus dipped into a sewer grate, managing to grab hold of the horizontal metal guide pole before falling into her lap.

Taking the second to last seat on the right side, Guy reached into the left side pocket of his Old Navy cargo shorts and retrieved his copy of *The Wars* by Timothy Findley. After thumbing through a few pages, he found the latest dog-ear and started reading.

Moments later, however, he set the book aside, his attention distracted by the elderly woman. She'd started talking to herself as soon as the bus pulled away from the stop, her words accompanied by a wide array of facial expressions, hand gestures, and repeated attempts to button her yellow cardigan.

Unfortunately, for Guy, the groaning bus engine and rattling windows made it impossible to hear what the woman was saying and he gave up trying, deciding instead to gaze out the window, his eyes cruising the various scenes occurring in Victoria Park — a baseball game, a family picnic, a game of bocce ball, and what looked to be a lovers' spat.

When the bus stopped at Dundurn Street to pick up a few more passengers, Guy spent a moment or two looking through the window directly across the aisle from him, noting what fell within its frame, before switching to the next window, then the next, then the next, as though he were quickly changing channels on a TV, pausing only when he reached the sixth window-channel, his attention piqued by the big black 'X' painted on the large billboard in the Fortinos Plaza, as though it was crossing out the underlying car advertisement.

Smiling, he thought of something Sadie had said on the way back from an Earth First! meeting: that the only thing she detested about taking the bus everywhere was having to look at all the cars travelling beside it.

He sighed, thinking how much easier and less complicated his life would be if he could date Sadie, if he could go to Montreal with her next weekend. But he couldn't. The thought of going back to Montreal, of bumping into someone he —

"Mr. Boucher? Is that you?"

Guy stopped breathing. The voice had come from beside him. Vaguely familiar, it wasn't so much the voice as the 'Mr. Boucher' that had caused Guy to stop breathing. He hadn't been called 'Mr. Boucher' since he quit teaching more than five years ago.

"Oh my God, it *is* you," the voice said.

When Guy looked up he saw Renaldo Ramiriz, an ex-student,

standing beside him, smiling, his brilliant white teeth gleaming. "I almost didn't recognize you with that fedora."

Guy smiled politely, said, "Hello," then picked up his book and was about to pretend to start reading it when Renaldo said, "It's me, Mr. Boucher. Renaldo Ramiriz. Remember? From Montreal? You were my teacher."

Guy nodded, smiling, making it appear as though he was trying to remember Renaldo. "Oh yes, I remember now."

"My God, what's it been, like, ten years?"

"Something like that."

"This is incredible. *Quelle surprise, n'est-ce pas?"*

Guy nodded. "Yes. Quite a surprise."

Renaldo was just as Guy had pictured him these past ten years: achingly handsome face; riveting cheekbones; smooth, olive skin; sparkling eyes; full, moist, crimson lips.

"I can't believe this," Renaldo said, slapping the back of the seat beside him. "I mean, what are the chances of us meeting like this?"

"Pretty slim," Guy replied.

Renaldo nodded, "No kidding," he said, shaking his head. Then, after motioning in the direction of an equally attractive but slightly younger man now seated across from the elderly woman, he said, "I was just saying to Juan that we should do something bourgeois like hop on a bus and voila — here you are!"

"Well, that was quite . . . fortunate," Guy said, his gaze lingering on the attractive young man.

"My God, it's good to see you!" Renaldo shouted, then, smiling collegially and lowering his voice, he added, "By the way, I took your advice and went into teaching."

"Really? That's great. Where are you teaching?"

"Costa Rica."

"Oh, my," Guy said, setting his book down again on the seat. "And how'd you end up there?"

"One of those teacher recruiting fairs that come around to the universities. Since I'm both Catholic and fluent in Spanish, it was fairly easy to get a job. I've been teaching there for five years now."

"Enjoying it, are you?" Guy asked, once again glancing at the attractive young man seated across from the elderly woman.

"Love it. And you were right."

"About what?" Guy asked, returning his gaze to Renaldo.

"The benefit *packages* associated with teaching are incredible," he replied, turning around and motioning to the attractive young man to join them.

Pulling himself quickly out of the seat, the young man walked towards Guy and Renaldo, smiling, his thin hips immediately falling into synch with the swaying bus. Guy returned the young man's smile, immediately mesmerized by his shoulder length dark hair and mocha skin; his green eyes; his full, flushed lips; the ample bulge in his —

"This is my friend, Juan," Renaldo said, interrupting Guy's appraisal.

"Nice to meet you, Juan," Guy said, extending his hand.

The combination of Juan's smooth, delicate skin and his firm embrace of Guy's hand relayed a pleasurable twang up Guy's arm.

"Juan," Renaldo said, making a semi-flamboyant gesture, "*this* is my mentor, Mr. Boucher."

Guy, about to let go of Juan's hand, suddenly felt Juan's grip tightening and noticed the polite, formal expression on Juan's face had been replaced by a mixture of doubt, intrigue, and admiration.

"Not *the* . . ."

Renaldo nodded, smiling broadly. "The one and only."

"Oh my. It is such an honour to meet you," Juan said, bowing his head slightly, now cupping Guy's right hand with both of his. "Renaldo has told me all about you. You're an institution. A legend. You're the reason I got into teaching. When Renaldo told me how you had revived the ancient Greek tradition of educating and patronizing young boys in exchange for sexual relations with them, I couldn't imagine doing anything else with my life."

Guy scanned the bus patrons quickly, trying to determine who, if anyone, had overheard Juan.

"You think Montreal is full of possibility, Mr. Boucher, you should teach in Costa Rica," Renaldo said, placing his hand on Juan's firm buttock and gently squeezing it. "The boys down there are literally ripe for the picking."

Guy felt an exquisite throbbing in his groin, his thoughts immediately returning to Sadie's comments about having sex on a train. He'd been tempted to tell her that this was where *his* first sexual experience had occurred, relating how, the summer before grade eleven he'd just boarded a Via train in Nova Scotia, bound for Montreal, when a man easily twice Guy's age took a seat beside him and a few minutes later, as the train was pulling out of the station, casually placed his hand on Guy's leg and began to gently caress it, immediately causing jolts of excitement to vibrate up Guy's leg and into his —

"So, what are you guys doing here?" Guy asked, wanting to change the subject, to assuage the sudden ejaculation of erotic images spurting into his visual cortex.

"We're on vacation," Renaldo replied. "The school we were teaching at gets out in mid-June so we did some surfing for a week before flying back home to Montreal. We've been in Toronto for the last few days for Gay Pride week but when a friend told us there was a pretty good scene here in Hamilton we'd thought we'd come and check it out. Is that why you're here?"

Guy shook his head. "I live here now."

"You left Montreal? Why?"

Guy shrugged. "It became too . . . challenging."

"Wow, I thought you'd never leave."

"Well, you know, things happen," Guy replied.

"You're still teaching, though, aren't you?"

Guy shook his head. "No. Unfortunately I was . . . I quit. I haven't taught in over five years," he said, cringing, reviewing the memory.

It was only a matter of time before his not-so-secret reputation for seducing schoolboys in Nova Scotia made it to Montreal. When it arrived, just before Christmas holidays more than five years ago, he did something he thought he'd never do: he immediately packed up his belongings and left.

The next sixteen months had been the lowest of his life, hopping from city to city — Hull, Ottawa, Kanata, Kingston, Peterborough, Toronto — taking jobs in grocery or retail stores, going on extended heterosexual binges, desperately trying to change himself. But it was impossible. Young men and teaching, preferably in combination, were the only things he really enjoyed, the only things that gave his life any significant meaning.

"I can't believe you're not teaching," Renaldo said, shaking his head. "You were so good at it. You were the only teacher who inspired us, who actually made a difference in our lives. You were *such* a good teacher, Mr. Boucher."

"Well, not everyone saw it that way I'm afraid," Guy said, hearing the 'Next Stop' bell ring before feeling the bus slowing down, preparing to stop in front of Second Cup in Westdale.

"So, do you like living here?"

"Actually, yes, I do. It's really quite nice."

"And how's the *scene*?"

"Well, it's not, of course, as liberal as Montreal or Toronto, but it's getting there, and —"

"He should come to Costa Rica with us," Juan said, suddenly, causing he and Renaldo to gasp and exchange glances as though this was a fabulous idea.

"Oh my God, Juan, you're brilliant," Renaldo shouted and then, turning to Guy, he said, "Juan's right. You should, Mr. Boucher. You speak Spanish. You have tons of teaching experience. They'd *love* you down there."

"I don't know," Guy said, trying not to smile.

"Oh come on, Mr. Boucher, what's there to know?"

"Really, boys. I don't think it's such a good idea," Guy replied, noticing the elderly woman wearing the yellow cardigan was now standing at the top of the steps, waiting for the doors to open.

"Personally, I think it's a completely offensive idea," the elderly woman said, turning to face the three men and glaring at them for a full two seconds before slowly, deliberately, descending the steps of the bus.

To Be Continued . . .

fyi

"Oh, Agnes, you're absolutely horrible," the woman said to herself as she stepped off the bus. "There's no end to your antics, is there? Here these men are having a nice conversation and you have to go and interrupt it with one of your snide comments."

Agnes, who hadn't heard a word the three men spoke until turning her hearing aid back on just as one man was suggesting that a Mr. Boucher come to Costa Rica, shook her head, at once amused by the sight of the two younger men now blowing her kisses through the open bus window as it pulled away from the curb and intrigued by what she imagined to be a look of profound guilt on the face of the man wearing the fedora.

"Mr. Boucher, I presume," she said, once again chuckling to herself. Then, just as she was about to start walking across the intersection, Agnes realized she had no idea why she was standing where she was.

"Now, why did I get off at this stop?" she wondered aloud, peering through her glasses at the hodgepodge of tiny stores, cafés, and restaurants contained in Westdale Village, expecting to see something that would trigger a memory.

"Hopeless," she said to herself, after a few moments. "I might as well be in a different country. Everything looks foreign." And then, just as she was about to comment on how much had changed since she was a little girl, she recognized something — the Westdale Theatre — immediately feeling comforted by this vestige from her childhood.

"I wonder what's playing," Agnes said, moving a few steps in the direction of the theatre, straining to read the marquee.

Her eyesight had deteriorated considerably in the last few years.

"I should probably make an appointment to see the doctor sometime soon," she said as she neared the curb, continuing to speak as though she were now in the doctor's office, having her eyes examined. "During the day it's not so bad, as long as the light is good. Otherwise, I'm forever bumping into things. I swear, the last time my eldest son came to visit, he thought I'd been beaten. He kept staring at my legs. I was too embarrassed to tell him I'd had several run-ins with the coffee table."

Agnes chuckled, picturing the look of concern on her son's face. "He'll be wanting to ship me off to an old-age home soon, I imagine."

Arriving at the curb, Agnes, still unable to read the marquee, but unwilling to go any further, swatted her hand in the direction of the theatre. "Probably one of those action-adventure movies that are so popular nowadays," she said, before retracing her steps, returning to roughly the spot where she'd been standing when she got off the bus.

"Action-adventure," she scoffed, glaring reproachfully at a group of young people sitting on the patio at Second Cup. "You people should've been in Hamilton during the summer of '46. *Then* you would've tasted some real action-adventure."

The summer of '46 had been one of the hottest in Hamilton's history, a blanket of heat descending on the city in late June, setting the temperament for an incendiary summer full of union strikes, hostile picket lines, arrests, fighting, vandalism, and other inflammatory incidents.

"And then," Agnes said, moving towards a nearby bench, wanting to relieve the pain in her ankles and feet, "just when people thought things couldn't get any more dramatic, along comes Evelyn Dick."

Oh, how I wanted to follow in Evelyn's footsteps, Agnes thought. Not to be accused of murdering my child and dismembering my husband or sentenced to life imprisonment, but to be famous. To have the cameras clicking, lights flashing, and newspapermen from all over

North America rushing to Hamilton to write about me. To have thousands of people crowding the streets just to catch a glimpse of me and everyone shouting my name. To have men, by the dozens, courting me and wanting to take me on trips all over the world.

"I suppose it wasn't meant to be," Agnes said, sighing as she plopped down on the bench, the pain in her feet and ankles subsiding almost immediately.

She'd met her husband on November 22, 1945, the day the boys from Royal Hamilton Light Infantry — the 'Rileys,' as they were known then — arrived home from the war. Agnes married him a year later, gave birth to their first child when she was nineteen, their third when she was twenty-four. Her husband, hired at Westinghouse shortly after the strike of '46, worked for thirty-five years before dying of a heart attack eight months after he retired, leaving Agnes a widow two days before her fifty-eighth birthday.

"My, my. That seems like a lifetime ago now," Agnes mused, taking a few moments to smooth out an imaginary crease in her pants.

There had been many times since her husband's death that she'd thought she'd made a mistake, that she shouldn't have said 'Yes' to her first proposal of marriage.

"Of course, if I hadn't said 'Yes' I may not have had three beautiful children."

Two of her three children — the boys — had children of their own now. Both of them lived in Burlington, worked on Bay Street in Toronto, and came to visit Agnes on a monthly basis. Her only daughter, spurred on by Agnes' encouragement, had had a semi-successful career as a model and stage actress and now worked as a weather reporter in Calgary.

"Even so, I can't say I didn't sometimes wish my husband had had his heart attack earlier, when I was in my thirties or forties," Agnes said, now fiddling with the buttons on her cardigan. "Being single at fifty-eight was no picnic. Who wants to hire a fifty-eight-year-old woman?"

A few months after her husband's death, she began applying for jobs at places all over the city — Woolworths, Zellers, Sears, Eatons

— but no one could use her. She finally settled on volunteering at Henderson Hospital, where her three children were born. This lasted until she was forced to leave on account of her lapses in memory.

"I can't believe how often it fails me these days."

At one time she could recite every line from movies like *Gone With the Wind, A Streetcar Named Desire,* and *Rebel Without a Cause.* Nowadays, however, she was reduced to carrying around a notepad like a companion, having to jot down things the moment they came into her head for fear that they would be gone the next.

"My notepad, my heavens. Why didn't I think of it sooner?" Agnes said, beginning to rummage through her white Italian leather purse, a gift from her daughter.

"There it is," she said, pulling the notepad out and reading the first entry below the 'Things to Remember' title. "Pills," she said, referring to the medication for her rheumatoid arthritis. "Now how on earth could I forget my pills?"

"You still on the pill, Grandma?"

Agnes turned in the direction of the voice and saw a young girl dressed in a tight tank top, very short shorts, and sneakers standing on a skateboard beside another girl who was dressed more modestly in a floral patterned yellow sundress and black penny loafers.

Agnes eyed the young girl in the tank top suspiciously. "Aren't you supposed to be in school, young missy?"

"FYI, it's Saturday, Grandma," the girl replied.

"It is?" Agnes asked, looking at the young girl in the yellow sundress for confirmation.

"Yes, ma'am," the girl in the sundress replied.

"Oh, dear," said Agnes, embarrassed at having forgotten what day it was. "Of course it is. What was I thinking?"

"Going a bit senile, eh, Grandma?" the girl on the skateboard said, laughing.

Shrugging off her embarrassment, Agnes pointed her slightly gnarled index finger accusingly at the young girl on the skateboard. "How old are you, young missy?" she said, starting to rise off the bench.

"Old enough to know you don't need to be on the pill," the girl replied, stepping off her skateboard and kicking it up into her hands. "But young enough to easily get away from you and that ugly pointy finger of yours," she added, starting to run in the direction of Westdale Theatre before hopping on her skateboard and riding across Marion Avenue, laughing and jeering at Agnes, who had already stopped walking, realizing she couldn't chase after the young girl, let alone catch her.

"I'm sorry, ma'am," the girl in the yellow sundress said, lightly touching Agnes' arm, adding, "Oh, and she's thirteen years old, by the way," before running to catch up to the girl on the skateboard.

. . . . To Be Continued . . .

how old is old?

"That wasn't nice," Katie said when she'd caught up to Natasha in the parking lot in front of the Westdale Theatre.

"FYI, I was just joking around," Natasha replied, stepping off her skateboard and kicking it up into her left hand.

"I like elderly ladies," Katie said, looking back at the elderly woman now slowly making her way across the street towards the pharmacy. "I think they're cute."

"FYI, *old* ladies aren't cute, they're boring. All they ever talk about is the way things used to be back when they were growing up. And they're always getting sick and costing society money."

That sounded exactly like something Natasha's stepmother would say, Katie thought to herself. Natasha's stepmother only liked young people or people who acted and looked young because she was terrified of growing old. In fact, last week she told Katie and Natasha about her recurring dream of finding a magic anti-aging cream that instantly made her look fifteen years younger than her real age, which was thirty-three.

"What happens when you wake up and realize it was just a dream?" Katie had asked.

"Oh my God, it's sooo depressing," Natasha's stepmother replied, bursting into tears a few moments later, telling Katie how she loathed the idea of getting old, of looking like a wrinkled prune and having to wear adult diapers and drink her meals through a straw.

"You sound like your stepmother," Katie said to Natasha, who had just finished taking a hit from her asthma inhaler.

"Yeah, well, FYI, it's true," Natasha replied, stuffing the inhaler back into the front pocket of her short shorts. "And my stepmother should know. She works in a nursing home."

"And what happens when your stepmother gets old?"

"FYI, she's never getting old. She said she'd rather kill herself than get old."

"How old is old?"

"Huh?" Natasha replied.

"How old did your stepmother say she can get before she'd kill herself?"

Natasha shrugged. "I don't know."

"You should ask her."

"Why?"

"Because her answer might change the older she gets."

"Whatever," Natasha said, rolling her eyes before hopping back on her skateboard.

"I bet it does," Katie said.

"Yeah? And I bet the only reason you think old ladies are cute is because you have to live with one all the time," Natasha replied. And then, just as she gave herself a push forward, she turned back to Katie and said, "Just because you don't have any real parents doesn't mean you have to —"

"Watch out!" Katie screamed, lunging towards Natasha.

. . . . **To Be Continued . . .**

an excellent choice

"Oh my God! We almost hit that girl on the skateboard," Lauren shouted at Ben through the slightly opened visor of her cherry red Shoei motorcycle helmet, adding, after glancing back at the girl who was now being helped up by her friend, "If it wasn't for her friend yanking her off her skateboard, she probably would've been . . ."

Ben nodded his helmet. "I know," he said, lifting his visor and easing off the accelerator, the Suzuki GSXR 1100 slowing as they approached the bend in King Street just in front of MacNeil Baptist Church. "I wasn't kidding when I said driving a motorcycle is a lot different than driving a car. People just don't pay attention. You have to be so much more aware on a motorcycle."

"I'm starting to get the picture."

"Does that mean you're having second thoughts about getting your motorcycle licence this summer?"

"I'm way beyond having second thoughts," Lauren said. "I'm somewhere between my seventh and eighth thought now."

Ben laughed. "Hey, you want to grab something to eat before we play pool?"

He hadn't eaten since he and Lauren had had dinner last night at the Cornerstone restaurant in Caledonia, after they'd got back from a ride out to Port Dover.

"Sure," Lauren replied.

"Any suggestions?"

"How about The Pita Pit?"

Ben smiled. "You couldn't have told me that thirty seconds ago, huh?"

"You didn't ask until three seconds ago."

Braking smoothly, Ben geared the motorcycle down from third to first, waited for an oncoming car to pass and then made a quick U-turn just before the lights at King and Dalewood, smiling to himself as he felt Lauren squeezing his well-defined stomach, thankful he hadn't eaten that leftover lasagna last night when he had gotten back from dropping Lauren off at her apartment, opting instead to go to bed hungry, knowing his abs would be tight and hard in the morning.

Zipping back to Sterling Avenue, he made a quick left onto Sterling before pulling into the parking lot outside the Westdale United Church.

"Hey," Lauren said, taking off her helmet and setting it on the motorcycle seat, "do you mind if I make a quick detour to the bookstore before we get something to eat?"

"I *knew* it," Ben said, shaking his head while stuffing his black leather motorcycle gloves into his helmet.

"Knew what?" Lauren said, primping her chestnut brown hair.

"I knew there had to be a reason we were stopping at The Pita Pit."

"You mean aside from the fact that they make great pitas?"

"Yeah," Ben replied, shaking his head. "They're close to the bookstore."

Lauren smiled. "Alright, I confess."

"I knew it."

"So, do you mind?"

"Mind what?"

"If I make a quick detour."

"Lauren, you and I both know there is no such thing as a quote-unquote *quick detour* where you and a bookstore are concerned."

"Is that so, mister?" she said, pulling a twenty-dollar bill from the back pocket of her velvet stretch pants. "In that case, I'll make you a deal. If you go and order me a bottled water and a chicken breast pita with everything on it and whatever you want for yourself, I'll bet you I meet you back at The Pita Pit before they're done making them."

Scooping up Lauren's helmet from the motorcycle seat and starting to walk across the street towards The Pita Pit, Ben smiled and said, "And what if you're late?"

"Then lunch *and* pool are on me."

"You know you're obsessed, don't you?"

"Do we have a deal?"

Ben hesitated, then, snatching the twenty-dollar bill from her hand, he said, "Lady, you got yourself a deal," before darting towards the entrance to The Pita Pit.

As soon as Ben snatched the twenty-dollar bill from her, Lauren started running down the sidewalk, slicing between two people then slaloming through three other people before dashing around the corner past The Adventure Attic and through the open doorway of Bryan Prince Bookseller — her forward progress immediately arrested by the sight of all the new books just waiting to be plucked off the shelves and given a new home.

Ben was right, she was obsessed. But who wouldn't be? Like Emily Dickinson had said, 'There is no frigate like a book to take us Lands away.' Reading books was the one thing Lauren wished Ben would do, aside from being able to speak French and not being so preoccupied with his abs. He was a TV person and had to have his RDA of *Will & Grace*, *Everybody Loves Raymond*, *ER*, *Law & Order*, *CSI*, and, of course, the latest reality show.

It wasn't that Lauren abhorred TV, she enjoyed an episode of *ER* or *CSI* as much as the next person, it was just that she loved reading — loved lying in bed on the weekends with a cup of tea and reading the morning away; loved reading in bed at night (she couldn't fall asleep without reading at least a chapter); loved reading on her commute back and forth to Toronto on the GO train; loved reading while waiting for Ben to come over.

Lauren breathed in the slightly sweet scent of the bookstore, setting in motion a panoply of memories of past visits to the store. She'd long ago noticed that every bookstore had its own particular smell; that Book City on Bloor West was different from Book City on Queen East; that Chapters in Ancaster was different from Chapters in Toronto; that Different Drummer in Burlington was different from Bryan Prince in Hamilton.

She breathed in again, this time the smell transforming the space into something sublime, causing her to wonder if this was how painters felt when entering the Sistine Chapel. I wish I could bottle this smell, she said to herself. I'd bathe in it or spray it on me whenever I needed a —

"Is there something I can help you find?"

It was one of the staff. Lauren had seen her many times before, enjoyed hearing her and the other staff discussing or reviewing the various books they'd read.

"It's Tracey, right?" Lauren said, smiling.

"Yes. How'd you know?"

"I overheard it the last time I was in. I'm Lauren, by the way," Lauren said, offering Tracey her hand.

"Nice to meet you, Lauren," Tracey said. "So, is there something specific you're looking for?"

"Um, no, not really. I'm just going to browse around a bit and wait until something jumps out at me, if that's okay."

"Of course. Browse 'til your heart's content."

"Thank you. It was nice meeting you."

"You too."

Lauren turned back to face the books, her eyes slowly trawling through the various sections, her hands occasionally reaching out to caress the spine of a particular book until, after reaching the fiction section she closed her eyes and gently passed her fingertips an inch or two above a row of books for a few moments before her hand suddenly fell forward and she plucked a book off the shelf.

"An excellent choice," she heard a voice — soothing and masculine — say before she opened her eyes.

Opening her eyes, Lauren saw the voice was attached to a tall, ruggedly handsome man with short dark hair and green eyes who looked as though he'd just walked out of a rock-climbing advertisement. In what Lauren guessed to be his mid- to late-twenties, the man was wearing a beige short-sleeved collared shirt, taupe cargo shorts, hiking boots, a knapsack, and just the right amount of facial hair.

Without looking at what book she'd pulled from the shelf, Lauren replied, "Really?"

"Excellent, indeed," the man said, smiling, revealing a set of almost white, slightly crooked teeth that gave his face even more charm. "In fact, it's actually my favourite book."

"Really?" Lauren said, making a mental note not to use the word 'Really?' again during this conversation.

The man nodded. "I've read it eleven times."

"I thought I was the only one who did that."

"Did what?"

"Read the same book more than once."

The man smiled. "It's the only way you can come to fully understand and appreciate a book," he said. "Plus, in my humble opinion, each time I sit down to read it, I do so as a slightly different or, in some cases, a drastically different person. In which case, even though it's the same book I read two months or two years ago, it ends up reading completely different."

Lauren smiled. She couldn't believe what she was hearing. It was as though this man was reading her mind, giving a voice to her thoughts, thoughts she'd kept hidden from everyone, including Ben.

"Of course," the man continued, chuckling, "there are also those times when I read it for the exact opposite reason. There are times when my life feels as though it's about to come flying apart and all I want to do is attach myself to something stable and known and so I'll read it just to have something familiar to hold onto, you know?"

"I can't believe this."

"Can't believe what?"

"That's exactly, I mean, *exactly*, how I feel."

The man smiled. "Well, it would seem, then, that you and I are . . . *book*mates."

Lauren felt a warm flush rush up her neck, prickling her skin, and tried desperately to will the advancing colour to recede.

"The colour suits you," the man said.

"Excuse me?" Lauren replied, feeling the skin on her cheeks tingling.

"Natural rouge."

"Oh, right," Lauren said, realizing he was referring to her now-crimson face. "Well, I guess . . . I mean," Lauren said, fumbling for something to say, before bowing her head and noticing for the first time that the book she'd pulled off the shelf was Henry David Thoreau's *Walden.* Even though she'd never had an interest in reading it before, she knew that today she would buy it and begin reading it immediately, just as she knew Ben would shake his head when he saw it, making some comment about her being unable to leave a bookstore empty-handed.

"I'm serious," the man said. "Of course, that's not to say I suggest you go out and buy some rouge at the cosmetics counter. It's just when you come by it honestly, as part of, you know . . . well, I guess what I'm really trying to say is I think you look great as is."

"Thank you," Lauren said, a fresh wave of blush surging into her cheeks,

"En effet, vous êtes la femme la plus captivante que j'ai connu dans l'année," and, with that said, he smiled, turned around, and walked quickly out of the bookstore.

. . . . **To Be Continued . . .**

luck

It wasn't until he had passed a guy standing outside The Pita Pit holding two pitas in his left hand and cradling two motorcycle helmets containing a bottle of water and a can of Coke in his right arm that Keith realized he still had an as-yet-unpaid-for copy of Margaret Atwood's *Surfacing* in his hand.

After a moment's deliberation, he decided against returning to the bookstore, believing it would ruin the near-perfect encounter he'd just had with the woman, opting instead to continue walking along Sterling Avenue while making a mental note to return to Bryan Prince Bookseller before it closed.

Immediately after turning right on Dalewood Crescent, he began replaying the conversation he'd just had with the woman. By the time he'd passed his favourite house on this street — #93 — he'd made some subtle modifications to their conversation. Instead of trying to impress her with his compliment in French, he'd decided that a better approach may have been to point at the book in her hand and ask, "So, have you ever read *Walden*?"

"No. But it must be pretty good if you've read it eleven times."

"It is. It's one of those books that puts everything into perspective. I mean, here was this guy who one day decided to head off into the woods and build his own cabin in the middle of nowhere — almost completely isolated from other people — in an effort to live a really simple life."

"Sounds interesting."

"It's been my inspiration."

"For what?"

"Hmmm. Why don't we discuss it over a cup of coffee?"

"I'd like that."

From here, while perusing the larger homes along Oak Knoll Drive, Keith imagined the two of them walking over to The Bean Bar or to Second Cup or even just across the street to TCBY and continuing their conversation.

By the time Keith reached Churchill Park and was walking down the path en route to the South Shore Trails of Cootes Paradise, he and the woman from the bookstore had progressed from having a coffee at TCBY to having dinner at The Snooty Fox and were just about to enter the Westdale Theatre to see an early movie, when the words, "You're not exactly an attractive catch, Keith," spoken by his twin sister at their birthday party four weeks ago, interrupted him. "I mean, sure, you're good-looking enough," his sister had gone on to say, "but that's pretty much where it ends. You don't have a car, a house, a job, a bank account. You don't even have your own apartment, for God's sake. You're living in your buddy's basement in a room the size of a walk-in closet. And your entire life can fit inside that stupid knapsack you're always carrying around with you. I mean, I realize the whole vagabond thing worked wonders when you were in your late teens and early twenties, but at thirty-seven, I'm not so sure women find it all that intriguing."

His sister was right, about almost everything. What she was wrong about was his current residence. He no longer resided in his buddy's basement. His buddy had moved out over two and a half months ago, rendering Keith homeless. For a while, he took turns staying at another friend's house, The Salvation Army, and the YMCA. Then, when the weather got warmer, he started spending more time outside — occasionally sleeping in parks — until one day, after re-reading *Walden* for the eleventh time, he got an idea.

"Beautiful day, isn't it?"

"Yes it is," Keith replied without thinking, abruptly pausing in mid-stride when he noticed the voice belonged to a thin, elderly man standing just off to the left of the small concrete bridge Keith had just crossed.

Wearing a very worn-in beige barn jacket, a brown T-shirt, and light brown overalls, the elderly man was holding a pair of overly worn brown Birkenstock sandals in his left hand and a leash attached to a golden retriever in his right.

It was not the first time Keith had seen the man and his dog. He'd spotted him dozens of times before, walking through Churchill Park or along the trails behind McMaster University. Sometimes they were joined by a young girl, presumably the man's granddaughter.

"Lovely day for a walk," Keith said, bending over to pet the man's dog.

Normally, Keith didn't initiate conversation with people walking in the park or on the trails and even avoided eye contact in an attempt to keep a low profile.

The elderly man nodded. "Indeed. Out for a stroll yourself, are you?"

Keith shook his head. "No, just taking a shortcut to the university."

"Summer classes?"

Keith hesitated, then nodded, thinking it was easier this way.

"Best time of your life, eh?"

"Excuse me?" Keith said.

"Isn't that what they say about university, that it's the best time of your life?"

Keith smiled. "So they say."

"You don't sound convinced."

"Oh, no, I'm enjoying myself. Can't complain."

"Well, I take it if you're walking to school, you must live close by."

"Pretty close."

"I just live over on South Oval, myself."

"That's a nice street."

The elderly man smiled. "I enjoy it. Some of my neighbours don't like it all that much. Too many students around. But I don't mind. It keeps me young."

Keith chuckled. "That's a good philosophy."

"As good as the next one, I suppose. Well, young man, I guess I shouldn't keep you from your education. Best of luck with your studies."

"Thank you. I need all the luck I can get," Keith said, smiling at the irony of his comment, before giving the man's dog a playful pat on the head and continuing down the trail.

To Be Continued . . .

guardian

"He's not fooling us, is he, Lucky?" Norman said to his dog, turning to watch the man walking down the path. "If he's a student, I'm the president of the university. In fact, I'll bet he's at least thirty-five if he's a day. And as for him living around here, now that I *don't* doubt. It's just a matter of which park bench he calls home."

After watching the man for a few more moments, Norman turned around and began making his way slowly, thoughtfully, in the direction of the small concrete bridge, enjoying the sensation of the moist path cushioning his footfalls, the damp earth occasionally squishing between his toes.

Norman had spent a good deal of his life walking, hiking, studying, and exploring Cootes Paradise. He knew almost every type of animal, bird, tree, insect, and soil that called this place home — and, just as his grandmother had done for him when he was a boy, he was now passing this information down to his granddaughter, sitting with her for hours, keenly observing the forest and all its inhabitants going about their daily activities.

Although several signs at the entrances and along the trails indicated that this area was managed by The Royal Botanical Gardens, Norman fancied himself the guardian of Cootes Paradise. As its guardian, he felt an obligation to explore any aberration of activity occurring within its boundaries and, although he wasn't sure what the not-so-young man pretending to be a student was up to, he knew the man spent a great deal of time in the forest, entering and exiting at various points and times, sometimes arriving with a knapsack and departing without one or departing with a completely different set of clothes than the set he had arrived with. Although Norman had a hunch what was going on, he was resolved to confirm or disprove this hunch before the end of the day.

"We'll find out what he's up to, won't we Lucky?" he said, bending over to pet the dog.

Lucky barked.

"That's my boy."

Just after crossing the small concrete bridge, Norman paused to drop his Birkenstocks to the ground, stepping into them before starting to quickly climb the hill. After over a minute of climbing, Norman paused at the top of the hill to check his heart rate, waiting for the second hand to get around to the twelve before counting off thirty beats in fifteen seconds, a mere one hundred and twenty beats per minute.

"Not bad for a sixty-seven-year-old man," he said to Lucky, recalling the check-up he'd had last month, where his doctor said he was in better shape than most forty-five-year-old men.

"And most six-year-old dogs, I see," Norman said, chuckling as he watched Lucky collapse in the shade of a nearby spruce tree.

The day after his daughter's funeral four years ago, Norman quit drinking and smoking and began exercising more, realizing he now had a responsibility to ensure he remained in good physical health.

After wiping his brow with the sleeve of his barn jacket, he glanced at his watch again before giving Lucky's leash a slight tug to warn the dog it was time to get up. When Lucky rose reluctantly to his feet, Norman continued walking, settling in at a brisk pace, estimating that he'd be home by no later than 2:15 p.m. — 2:20 p.m. if he made a short detour to pick up a coffee at Tim Horton's, which would still be ten minutes before the time he'd agreed to meet his granddaughter for their regular —

"Norman!"

To Be Continued . . .

a lost art

Jessica had seen Norman and Lucky walking across Churchill Park just as she and Jason were about to make a right onto Oak Knoll Drive and immediately suggested to Jason that they go over and say hello.

"You're going to love him," she'd told Jason as they cycled towards Norman. "He's this quirky old guy that lives a couple houses down from me with his wife and granddaughter."

"Granddaughter?"

"Yeah, her parents were killed in a car crash four years ago so they're raising her."

"How old are they?"

"I don't know. Sixty-five, maybe a little older. But they're awesome people. Great neighbours. They'll do anything for you. You know how some people have like 'No Trespassing' or 'Private Property' or 'Do Not Walk on the Grass' signs planted in their front lawns? Well, they have this sign in big, bold letters on their front lawn that says, 'PLEASE WALK, SIT, AND/OR PLAY ON THE GRASS — ANYTIME!' And two summers ago they put a couple of benches on their front lawn right next to the sidewalk and engraved them with, 'For those in need of temporary repose.'"

Jason chuckled. "That's cool."

"I know. Oh, and get this, they *homeschool* their granddaughter."

"No way, really?"

Jessica nodded. "He and his wife are retired school teachers and they take turns teaching her Monday through Saturday."

"Six days a week?"

"You should meet their granddaughter. She's scary smart."

"That's so cool."

"I know, it's — okay, shhh, here he is," Jessica said, applying the brakes on her CCM mountain bike. "Hi, Norman."

Norman smiled. "And how is my favourite Ph.D. candidate doing today?"

"Great, thanks," Jessica replied, smiling. "Norman, this is my friend Jason Starkman. Jason, this is my neighbour, Norman Holland."

"Pleased to meet you, sir," Jason said, offering his hand.

"Nice to meet you, too, Jason," Norman replied, shaking Jason's hand. "You wouldn't happen to be a descendant of Bessie Starkman, would you?"

"You mean Bessie Perri, don't you?"

"I see you know your local history, my boy."

Jason smiled. "I'm a fourth generation Hamiltonian," he said. "I heard all the stories growing up. But no, we're not related."

"Who's Bessie Starkman . . . er . . . Perri?," Jessica asked, feeling a little left out of the conversation.

Norman and Jason looked at each other, as if to give the other the chance to respond before Norman gestured to Jason and said, "The stage is yours, my boy."

Jason bowed slightly in Norman's direction then turned to Jessica and said, "Bessie Starkman married Rocco Perri and they ran the most infamous bootlegging gang in Canada during the conscription years."

"My father was around during those years," Norman chimed in. "He used to see the Perri gang zipping around Hamilton in their souped-up delivery trucks making the rounds. Everyone used to love the Perri gang back then."

"Everyone but the Protestants," Jason said.

"True enough," Norman said, chuckling. "True enough."

"Hey, this is quite a nice dog you have here," said Jason, bending over to pet Lucky.

Norman smiled. "Hear that, boy?" he said, giving the leash a light tug. "Master Jason here thinks you're nice."

Lucky barked.

"Well, I'm certain if he witnessed your table manners he might revise his opinion of you."

Jason and Jessica laughed.

"So, where are you folks off to today?" Norman asked.

"We're on our way to The Bean Bar," Jessica replied.

"Oh, yes. The restaurant right beside The Westdale Theatre. I walk by it nearly every day on my way to the park. I've never been in. Mind you, it looks like a nice enough place."

"It is," said Jessica.

"Great venue for conversations," added Jason.

"Is that the reason you're going there?"

"We're actually meeting up with a few of our old roommates from McMaster," Jessica said. "It's a reunion of sorts."

"Is that so?"

Jessica nodded. "After graduating a few years ago, we promised each other we'd get together every year the last Friday in June to catch up. This will be the fourth year we've done it."

"Good for you," Norman said, smiling. "And here I was telling my wife a while ago that conversation was a lost art. You know, I remember a time when that was what we did for entertainment. We would have people over to our house or go out to a restaurant for the sole purpose of having a good conversation. My wife and I found nothing more invigorating. It's good to see the two of you carrying on the tradition."

"We're trying," Jessica said.

"Well, if you'll excuse me," Norman said, tipping an imaginary hat to Jason and Jessica, "I should be going. I promised my granddaughter a hike in the woods and if I don't get home soon, she and my wife will be wondering where I wandered off to."

"Okay. Well, it was nice to see you again, Norman."

"Always a pleasure to see you, Ms. Jessica. And it was nice to meet you, Master Jason. I hope the reunion conversation is a big success."

"Thanks, Norman," Jessica replied, starting to pedal away. "I'll see you later."

"It was nice to meet you, too, sir," Jason said, shaking Norman's hand and petting Lucky a couple more times before turning his bike around and following Jessica.

"Well?" Jessica asked when Jason had caught up to her.

Jason chuckled. "You were totally right. He's awesome. I'd love to have him as my grandfather."

"Yeah. He's pretty cool," Jessica said, throwing a final glance over her shoulder at Norman, smiling when she saw him standing at the edge of the park, holding Lucky's leash, and giving the thumbs-up sign to a black BMW as the sound of Sarah McLachlan's song "Ice Cream" filled the park.

. . . . **To Be Continued . . .**

shut your bloody yaps . . . .

"Okay, was that my imagination or did that old man just give us the thumbs up?" Lucinda asked, taking her right hand off the steering wheel and turning down the volume on the stereo.

"No, he definitely gave us the thumbs up," Lance replied, looking in the side-view mirror in an attempt to locate the man.

"That's priceless."

"He must be a Sarah McLachlan fan."

"Must be."

Lance smiled, now watching the old man crossing the street behind them, wondering if, when he was his age, he'd be giving young people the thumbs up as they drove by.

"I can't get over how much the university has changed," Lance said, losing sight of the old man as Lucinda negotiated the near hairpin corner that changed Dromore Crescent into Marion Avenue North. "Every year it seems as though another building or residence goes up and totally changes the skyline of the entire campus."

"I know, it's thoroughly disconcerting," Lucinda said, nodding her head.

"Excuse me, but did I just hear you say, 'thoroughly disconcerting'?"

"Yeah, so?"

"Wow, can I ever tell we're about to see Rawnie again."

"Why do you say that?"

"Because you're starting to use polysyllabic words," Lance replied, his eyes now scanning the bowlers playing at Churchill Lawn Bowling

Club, admiring their white uniforms and wondering how old a person had to be to join such a club.

"I always talk like this."

Lance smiled. "No, you don't. You only break out the big words when we're going to meet Rawnie."

"Fuck you."

"Now that's more like it."

A few seconds later, after pulling her car into a recently vacated parking space on North Oval Street and hitting the POWER button on the car stereo, Lucinda said, "Well, all I can say is, I hope Rawnie isn't in one of her moods."

Lance chuckled. "Luce, Rawnie is *always* in one of her moods. You just have to learn to deal with it."

"I shouldn't have to. I mean, why should she be pissed off at me because I ended up being successful and she ended up being, well, whatever it is she is."

"Luce, I don't think Rawnie's pissed off at you for being successful."

"Yeah, well, this time around I'm not putting up with her condescension. If she starts being that way with us again, I'm going to tell her to shut up."

"You go, girl."

"I mean it."

"So do I."

"Okay," Lucinda said, taking a quick peek at herself in the rearview mirror. "How do I look?"

After glancing at Lucinda's Antonio Melani Derby shoes (with matching Antonio Melani handbag), her Banana Republic beige linen pants, her Marc Jacobs white cotton blouse, and her impeccable makeup, Lance, despite thinking, as he always did, that Lucinda looked like a considerably younger and more commercialized version of Gloria Steinem, said, "Fucking fabulous, girlfriend."

"Thank you. Okay, let's go," Lucinda said, getting out of the car and primping her hair before arming the car alarm and walking in the direction of The Bean Bar.

■ ■ ■

The large front windows of The Bean Bar were open, allowing a heavy spray of sunlight and the warm afternoon breeze to penetrate deep inside the interior of the café. Temporarily distracted by the aromatic fusion of herbal teas, coffees, and decadent desserts, it took a few moments before Lance noticed a pair of waving arms at the back of the bar, just past the main serving island. Thirty seconds later, after exchanging hugs and 'It's-so-good-to-see-you-again' comments with Jason and Jessica, he and Lucinda took a seat at the table.

"Did you guys order already?" Lance asked.

Jason shook his head. "We just got here, like maybe two minutes before you guys."

"Rawnie not here yet?" Lucinda inquired, making a quick visual sweep of the café.

"In the bathroom," Jason replied, throwing his thumb behind him in the direction of the doorway leading to the washrooms downstairs.

"And how is *she* doing?"

Jason shrugged. "Couldn't tell you. She came in maybe thirty seconds before you guys, said 'Hi' to us in mid-stride and went straight to the washroom."

"Typical," Lucinda said.

"So, did you two have your usual tour of the university before coming here?" Jessica asked, causing Lance to smile.

Jessica was the mediator of the group and spent a good deal of her time trying to re-direct Lucinda and Rawnie to 'safer' topics. Jessica obviously didn't want this to turn out the way it did last year, with Lucinda and Rawnie getting into a heated argument and the rest of them remaining mute for fear of being accused of choosing sides.

"Yes," Lucinda said, her eyes still on the doorway leading to the washrooms, "we took a quick walk through campus a while ago."

"Anything to report?" Jason asked.

"Yeah," Lance said. "I can't get over how much McMaster changes from year to year. I was just telling Luce how it seems like there's a new building or two going up every year."

"Well, isn't McMaster's slogan, 'Changing tomorrow today'?" Jessica asked.

"It used to be," Jason said. "But they changed it."

Lance smiled. "C'est la vie."

"True enough," Jason replied. "I mean, even this place has changed," he said, feeling an unexpected twinge of nostalgia for the couches and coffee table and magazine rack that had been replaced by the new end bar.

"Speaking of changes," Jessica said, stealing a quick glance at Jason. "Have you heard?"

"Heard what?" Lance asked.

"About Jason's change of career?"

"Oh my God, really?" Lucinda said, removing her gaze from the doorway leading to the bathroom and looking at Jason in disbelief. "What is it this time?"

Jason smiled. "Ladies and gentleman, you're looking at a bona fide, dyed-in-the-wool-suit, pharmaceutical rep," he said, before bowing his head.

"What happened to Chiropractic College?"

"I dropped out."

"Why?"

"Wasn't for me."

"That's what you said about Med school."

"I know."

Lance chuckled. "This is like, what, the fourth career change in as many years for you?"

"Well, let's see," Lucinda said before Jason could answer. "He got into Med school but postponed it to go to Law school. Then he dropped Law after a few months and enrolled in Med school for a year. Then he dropped out of that and went to Chiropractic College. And now he's a pharmaceutical rep — all in almost exactly four years. Jason, that's just —"

"Incredibly stupid."

The statement belonged to Rawnie DeVrais, who was now approaching the table, smiling.

"So much for formalities," Lance said, clapping his hands together as Rawnie sat herself beside Jason, across the table from Lucinda and Lance. "Mesdames et Messieurs, let the conversation begin!"

Rawnie laughed. "How's the gay life treating you, Lance Romance?" she said, winking at him.

"Can't complain."

"You look good."

"Thank you. So do you," Lance replied. "And I'm not just saying that. I swear if I weren't gay, Lucifer himself couldn't keep me from trying to win your heart."

Everyone laughed. Except Lucinda, who rolled her eyes and gave Lance a light kick under the table with her Melani shoes.

"You still diggin' the whole Toronto scene?" Rawnie asked Lance.

Lance nodded. "Still diggin' it."

"Going to be in the Gay Pride Parade again this year?"

"Of course. Wouldn't miss it. Third largest pride parade in the world."

"You and your boyfriends got your float ready?"

"Almost. They're just putting the finishing touches on it today," Lance said, and then, looking around at the others, he added, "The parade's tomorrow, you know, guys. If anyone's interested I can probably get you on the float with us."

"You should take Jason with you," Rawnie said. "He's switched careers so often in the last few years, he'd probably come back from the parade a switch-hitter."

Jason laughed. "You never know."

"Seriously though," Lance said, giving Jason a playful nudge, "what's up with all the career changes?"

Jason shrugged. "I don't know."

"It's the same problem he has in his relationships," Jessica blurted. "Fear of commitment."

"Jessica."

"Well, it's true, Jason. I mean, come on. What's your longest relationship, two weeks?"

"She does have a point," Rawnie said.

"Do you have anything to say in your defence, Mr. Starkman?" Lance said, adopting a formal-sounding voice.

Smiling, Jason cleared his throat and said, "Only that I'm a product of the Sega-Nintendo/ A.D.H.D./ I-need-it-right-now/ I'm-over-bored-with-everything-immediately/ that-is-so-ten-minutes-ago/ if-I-commit-to-this-I-might-miss-out-on-something-twice-as-good generation, so it should come as no surprise to anyone here that I can't stick with something longer than a few weeks."

"Oh please," Jessica said. "Don't even try that shit with us."

"Hey, I'm the victim here. Me. I didn't ask to be born into this world. I didn't ask my parents to raise me in the 'Jason-gets-whatever-Jason-wants' way they did. I had no choice, no say in the matter. Which is why I blame them and, beyond them, society at large for the way I turned out."

By this time everyone was laughing, including Lucinda, who, Lance noticed, was now giving Rawnie a thorough examination, undoubtedly noting, as he had moments earlier, that Rawnie was sporting unwashed, uncombed, and unstyled hair; no make-up; no jewellery; and, because it was Saturday, her Tuesday-Thursday-Saturday summer outfit, which consisted of a pair of re-stitched, re-styled, slightly tattered blue jeans and a handmade beige V-neck hemp shirt — the exact same outfit she was wearing last year when they'd all met.

When Lucinda curled her lip ever so slightly, betraying her profound disapproval of Rawnie's fashion sense, Lance couldn't help but smile. He'd heard the story many times before, how Lucinda and Rawnie had been best friends since grade school; how one day Rawnie, according to Lucinda, suddenly changed, returning to their student house and telling Lucinda she'd dropped out of Business and enrolled in Peace Studies at McMaster University; how Lucinda felt betrayed — not only because Rawnie hadn't even bothered to tell her beforehand, but also because it ruined their dream of moving to Oakville and opening their own fashion boutique, something they'd been talking about doing since high school. Of course, Lance also knew Lucinda secretly admired Rawnie for the change, just as he knew she despised the fact that Rawnie could look so good without make-up or expensive designer clothes.

"Finished your examination yet?" Rawnie asked, turning her head slowly in Lucinda's direction, an amused expression on her face.

"Almost," Lucinda replied, matter-of-factly, recovering, Lance thought, very nicely for someone who'd just been caught checking out what her competition was wearing. "I noticed your outfit is the same as last year's and I was just about to see what you were wearing on your feet."

Rawnie lifted her leg and slammed her sandals on the table.

"Same ones as last year?"

Rawnie nodded. "Would you like me to get you a pair?"

"No, that's okay," Lucinda replied, shaking her head. "I prefer to change my fashion style every once in a while."

"Ah, but you see, my dear Lucinda, *that* is where you err. It is not *your* style."

Lucinda made an expression as if to suggest that what Rawnie had said couldn't be further from the truth. "Sure it is."

"Oh no, it's not. You see, if it was *your* style, you'd have more than likely made the clothes yourself. However, since you didn't make the clothes yourself, nor did you get someone else to make them for you, you're just buying what some designer in Paris or New York or Toronto decided was going to be in style."

"Are you any different?"

"Well, yeah. I mean, aside from not having bought a single new 'off-the-rack' outfit in I don't remember how many years, I not only shop at The Salvation Army and Goodwill, but I make or alter most of what I wear into my own style. Of course, I don't have a problem with the fact that you have neither the creativity nor the ambition to do this and therefore have to rely on others to create your style."

"Damn, it's good to see you guys again," Lance said, emphatically. "Really, it is. I just love this stuff."

"So, are you saying that because we don't make our own clothes, we don't have any creativity?" Jessica asked.

"No, no, it's not that. Well, maybe, yeah. I mean, for God's sake, Jessica, look at you guys. In fact, look at everyone in this place. You all look like a bunch of carbon copies. I feel like I'm trapped inside a Gap commercial or a Banana Republic advertisement. I mean, this is precisely why Al-Quaeda hijacked those airplanes and flew them into the World Trade Center and the Pentagon."

"What?"

"Nice link," said Jason.

"Wait a second, I'm lost. You're saying that us not making our own clothes is responsible for 9/11?"

"Possibly," Jason replied, chuckling, before going on to say, "I know I shouldn't speak for Rawnie, but I think what she's getting at is for the last sixty or seventy years the U.S. has forcefully exported their lifestyle, culture, fashion, values, beliefs, etcetera, to the rest of the world and in the process contributed to the slow deterioration or, in some cases, the rapid destruction of the lifestyles, culture, fashion, values, and beliefs of countless other nations, which has fostered a hell of a lot of resentment and backlash."

"Couldn't have said it better myself," Rawnie said, smiling at Jason.

At this point in the conversation, Lance stood up, slid his chair to the side, and, after glancing behind him and taking one step backwards, executed a perfect back somersault before sitting down again at the table.

"What the hell was that for?" Lucinda asked.

"He's trying to prove he's not a carbon copy," Jessica said.

Lance smiled. "Actually, I'm just so happy to be here with you guys again, listening to us talk just like we used to, that I had to do something to express it. And there's only so many times you can say, 'Damn, it's good to see you guys,' before it loses its effect."

"Lance, you're one in 6.5 billion."

"Thanks, Rawnie. And you know something, for the most part, I agree with you and Jason about the inherent dangers and obvious backlash associated with the U.S. over-exporting their values, beliefs, and culture, etcetera. But what you said about how if we're not making or designing our own clothes it's because we don't have the creativity — I don't think it's solely a creativity issue. In fact, I think it's more of a time issue than anything else. We simply don't have time to sit down and design or make our own clothes like we once did. We're too busy doing other things."

"I second that sentiment," Lucinda said, nodding her head.

"I third it," said Jessica. "Everyone I know barely has enough time to shop for food these days, never mind clothes."

Lucinda nodded. "It's like our lives are on fast forward, like there's never enough time to do the things you want to."

"Exactly," Jessica said, pointing at Lucinda. "It's as though we're all running around like we're fifteen minutes late for our fifteen minutes of fame."

"You know what we need?" Lance said, clapping his hands.

"What?" Lucinda asked.

"A good dose of seventeenth-century realism. Erase a few centuries of technological advancement and we'd live a much less hectic life."

"Yeah," Lucinda replied, rolling her eyes at Lance's suggestion, "and a considerably shorter one full of pain and disease, where something as simple as the measles or chicken pox or a toothache ends up killing you."

"You ever wonder why we feel like there's never enough time?" Jason said, moving slightly forward in his seat.

Smiling, Lance shook his head. "Please, o' wise one, tell us."

"Well, part of the problem is that our mechanical and external information processing and delivery systems have sped up exponentially but *we* haven't. We've remained relatively fixed. So, even though we're being exposed to things that can communicate or interact instantaneously, our minds are still only able to process and grapple with things at the same speed."

"What are you talking about?"

"Okay, think of it this way. It wasn't that long ago that sitting down and writing a handwritten letter on a piece of paper, sticking it in an envelope, pasting a stamp on it, and slipping it into the nearest mailbox and having to wait a few days or a few weeks for it to arrive at its destination was the quickest way to communicate with someone via the printed word. Nowadays, however, we check our e-mail inbox from one minute to the next and find letters from all over the world in it, all of which have been delivered instantly."

"You know, it's really too bad the millennium Y2K thing never happened. It would've given people a wake-up call as to what's really important."

"Screw Y2K," Rawnie said. "What would really be cool is if one day all of us —"

"Shut your bloody yaps," Richard growled under his breath, suddenly gripped by an overwhelming urge to spit into his still-frothy mocha latte and then toss it in the direction of the five young people seated at the nearby table.

To Be Continued . . .

one of your episodes . . . .

"Excuse me?" Rheanne replied, looking up from smelling her Paradiso peach-flavoured tea.

"That table of five over there," Richard replied, motioning in the direction of the people he'd been listening to since he and Rheanne sat down five minutes ago. "Goddamn windbags, all of them. They remind me of a bunch of armchair commentators sitting around talking about things but never doing anything."

"Who knows?" Rheanne said, shrugging. "Maybe they are."

Richard sneered. "They're not."

"How can you be so sure? I mean, how do you know that they didn't decide to meet here with the specific intent of formulating some plan or strategy to do something about what they're discussing?"

"I can just tell."

"Richard, I'm sorry, but you cannot just tell. Besides, who are you to criticize them?"

"Hey, I was —"

"Exactly. You *were*. But I'm talking about recently. In the last year. Even in the last two years. What have you done that gives you the right to judge or criticize those five people for doing the same thing you've done these past couple of years? I mean, really, tell me what you've done that —"

As Rheanne continued speaking, her words made Richard feel like a traitor, forcing him, once again, to realize how much his life had changed in the past two years, how, although he now led a more socially acceptable lifestyle, it had come with a price. And that price was that he was now impotent to criticize others. "You're either part of the problem or part of the solution," he used to tell people, taking pride in the fact that his ecological footprint was microscopic, that if everyone lived the way he did, the Earth could be only half its size and still support its six billion plus inhabitants. Now, however, since he'd replaced his one bedroom apartment where everything was within walking distance with an oversized house in the suburbs where everything, including the corner store, required a car to get to, his ecological footprint was so large that if everyone lived like he did it would require 8.5 Earths to support the world's current population.

Damn, I miss my old life, he thought, once again glancing at the table of five. He especially missed the advantage of always being right, of always knowing he was speaking the truth when he told people about the ills of owning a vehicle, of living in the suburbs, of putting chemicals on their lawns, of patronizing golf courses. His life had meaning, direction, purpose. Most of all, he missed the fact that whenever he made a comment on the social or ecological impact of some activity, it wasn't immediately thrown back in his face by Rheanne telling him, "Richard, in case you need reminding, you're now part of the problem, too."

Speaking of Rheanne, he noticed she had stopped talking and was now staring at him, her face full of condescension. He couldn't believe he had allowed himself to fall in love with someone like her. Someone who shared so few of his values and beliefs.

"And how is everything here?"

It was the waiter, hovering over Richard's left shoulder, wearing a magnanimous expression, as though he had imparted some sort of everlasting bit of happiness and fulfilment on Richard and Rheanne by bringing them their drinks a few minutes earlier.

"Actually, it's altogether intolerable," Richard said, smiling serenely, barely able to contain himself.

"I'm . . . well, I mean . . ." the waiter stammered, frazzled by Richard's unexpected response. "Is there something wrong with —"

"With my life?" Richard said, cutting the waiter off in mid-sentence. "Funny you should ask. There is. Outward appearances to the contrary, my good man, I'm frustrated as hell and I'm not going to take it anymore."

"Richard, please," Rheanne whispered, her eyes narrowing, her brows furrowing the way they did whenever she was scolding him. "You're making a scene."

"No, Rheanne," Richard said, getting up from his seat and dropping a ten-dollar bill on the table, "I'm making an exit."

"Richard, what . . . why . . . what are you . . . Richard!"

But Richard only waved without looking back and continued to walk out of the café, already imagining himself selling his Passat, his house, his golf clubs. In fact, once he was outside and felt the warm sunlight on his face, he decided he would give away all his possessions except for maybe his old mountain bike. This idea — of ridding himself of all his excess junk — inspired him to raise his arms over his head and shout, "Free at last! Free at last! Thank God, Almighty, I'm free at —"

"— chard. Richard!"

It was Rheanne. She was staring at him. She looked concerned. Very concerned.

"Are you okay now?" she asked.

He noticed her hands were on his wrists, gently but firmly pinning his arms to the tabletop.

"What are you . . . why are your . . . what's going on?" he asked, confused.

"You were having another one of your episodes," Rheanne whispered.

"Another one of my —"

Richard stopped talking the moment he realized he was still in The Bean Bar, seated across the table from Rheanne, that he hadn't gotten up and stormed out of the café with one life-altering decision — that he'd had another of his episodes.

"Was it a bad one?" Richard asked.

"Bad enough," Rheanne replied, letting go of his wrists.

Richard sighed and buried his face in his hands. A few moments later, after apologizing to Rheanne, he slowly lifted his face out of his hands and made a quick survey of the café to see who else had noticed.

To Be Continued . . .

in the middle of something . . . .

Kalib44: Uh, oh. He's looking over here.

Summergalpal: Did he notice you?

Kalib44: I don't think so.

Summergalpal: So you were saying that this Richard guy was a bit of a nutbar?

Kalib44: Well, he wasn't really a nutbar.

Summergalpal: What was he then?

Kalib44: Well, he used to be one of those guys that went around chaining himself to trees to protest logging old growth forests, or going to places like Seattle and Quebec City to protest the WTO and NAFTA. Things like that.

Summergalpal: Well, that's pretty cool.

Kalib44: Yeah, I guess. The thing that wasn't so cool was that you couldn't really have a conversation with him because he'd always be having another conversation with himself.

Summergalpal: That's weird.

Kalib44: Yeah, that was Richard.

Summergalpal: Did you know him well?

Kalib44: No, not really. He only worked there for a month or so.

Summergalpal: I wonder who the woman he's with is?

Kalib44: Probably his therapist.

Summergalpal: Maybe they're on a date.

Kalib44: Maybe.

Summergalpal: Think they met on the Internet?

Kalib44: Speaking of which, what made you decide to do it?

Summergalpal: Do what?

Kalib44: Internet dating.

Summergalpal: I got tired of going to bars or mixers or parties and listening to guys feeding me bullshit lines all evening in hopes of getting some action.

Kalib44: LOL. Well, I wouldn't really classify the Internet as a medium for honesty. I mean, don't get me wrong, I'm all for making yourself look good but some of the stuff people write in their profiles goes way beyond little white lies.

Summergalpal: You don't have to warn me about the upsell. I know all about it. Trust me.

Kalib44: Had a few bad experiences have you?

Summergalpal: Let's just say there were a couple of guys who thought I'd be so captivated with their personality and pocket book that I'd forget the fact that they were physically not anything like they'd described in their profile.

Kalib44: Well, that's the problem with Internet dating — you don't get that immediate, 3-D, live-and-in-person person to check out.

Summergalpal: True enough.

Kalib44: So, how many Internet dates have you been on?

Summergalpal: You mean where I've actually met the guy?

Kalib44: Yeah.

Summergalpal: 6.

Kalib44: Wow. And you've only been doing this for 3 months?

Summergalpal: I don't like to waste my time. I figure if we make some sort of connection online there's no sense in waiting three weeks and writing 50 or 60 emails and having a bunch of IM sessions only to discover we have no physical chemistry.

Kalib44: Aren't you afraid of meeting some guy after only a few e-mails and him turning out to be a psycho?

Summergalpal: Please. I'm a lawyer and my older brother and my father are cops. Plus I always tell my brother where I'm going, who I'm meeting, and if I haven't called him within 10 minutes of when I'm supposed to, he comes looking for me.

Kalib44: LOL. Well, I guess you've got yourself covered.

Summergalpal: And then some. By the way, what does LOL mean again? I keep forgetting.

Kalib44: LOL = Laughing Out Loud.

Summergalpal: Thanks. I'm not even close to being fluent in Internet-language.

Kalib44: No worries. I just learned LOL last week. Anyway, how about it then?

Summergalpal: How about what?

Kalib44: How about us meeting?

Summergalpal: Well, I don't know . . .

Kalib44: What's that supposed to mean?

Summergalpal: Don't get me wrong, you seem intriguing enough, I just don't know if I'm up for being disappointed again. Are you sure you look like you say you do in your profile?

Kalib44: Well, almost.

Summergalpal: Almost?

Kalib44: Okay, the truth is, I'm not 6', 180 lbs, with green eyes and a thick head of wavy brown hair, I'm actually 5'2" tall, borderline obese, have brown eyes, a handlebar moustache and suffer from male pattern baldness.

Summergalpal: Haha . . . I find myself strangely attracted to the real you.

Kalib44: Well, since I'm being completely honest, I should probably tell you that I really don't own my own home but live in a two bedroom apartment with my mother and sister — both of whom are shut-ins and bipolar.

Summergalpal: Uh, oh. That brought you down a few notches.

Kalib44: I'm not done yet.

Summergalpal: Sorry, go on.

Kalib44: My hobbies include wearing flannel shirts, shaving my thick carpet of back hair, running with scissors, serial killing, searching for places to dispose of bodies, cleaning out the trunk of my Lexus and competing in — drum roll, please — Crazy 8s tournaments. How does that sound?

Summergalpal: You sound like EXACTLY the type of man my brother and father are looking for. LOL. (Hey, check me out with the Internet lingo!) As for me, although physically I think we might be compatible, I'm looking for someone with a little less baggage in his trunk.

Kalib44: I'm only kidding. Well, except for three of the aforementioned attributes. I'll leave you to wonder which three.

Summergalpal: Well, I certainly hope one of the three exceptions is Crazy 8s.

Kalib44: Are you a fan of Crazy 8s?

Summergalpal: Absolutely. I haven't played in years, though.

Kalib44: Well, it just so happens I have a deck of cards on me. Care to play a game?

Summergalpal: Just one?

Kalib44: Okay, how about the best two out of three?

Summergalpal: Want to make a wager?

Kalib44: I didn't take you for a gambler.

Summergalpal: It's not gambling if you have skills.

Kalib44: I like the confidence. So, does this mean you'd like to meet?

Summergalpal: I'm seriously considering it.

Kalib44: Trust me, you won't be disappointed. In all honesty, I'm not one of these persons using the relative anonymity of the Internet to dupe women into meeting him. In fact, this is probably my last attempt at Internet dating for a while.

Summergalpal: Really?

Kalib44: Yep. If things don't work out this time, I think I'll go back to the old fashioned way.

Summergalpal: Which is?

Kalib44: Meet them at a bar, slip a pill in their drink, take them back to the apartment and brainwash them into thinking they're my girlfriend until I get tired of them and then it's . . .

Summergalpal: It's into your trunk they go?

Kalib44: Precisely.

Summergalpal: LOL. So, where are you?

Kalib44: At a café.

Summergalpal: `Really? Wow, you must have a nice laptop.`

Kalib44: `It's actually a`

"Is that a wireless laptop?"

The voice, female, came from in front of Kalib.

"Um, yeah, it is," Kalib said, not looking up at the woman who had asked him the question, continuing to type his instant message on his laptop.

"Mind if I ask you how much you paid for it?" the woman asked.

"It actually belongs to my sister."

"No kidding? She must be pretty understanding. My sister used to freak out on me if I'd ask to borrow one of her CDs. I can't even imagine what she'd do if I asked to use her —"

"Listen, I'm kind of in the middle of something here," Kalib said, pointing at his laptop.

"Oh, okay. Sorry to disturb you," the woman said, smiling politely before starting to walk out of The Bean Bar, already retrieving her cell phone from the front pocket of her carpenter jeans and speed-dialling a pre-programmed phone number.

"Hi, J.P., it's Charmaine. How are you? That's good. I think — excuse me? Oh, fine, thanks. Well, actually, I think I've found something I'd really like to donate. Um, outside some place called The Bean Bar. Okay, I'll try my best, but you'd better hurry."

To Be Continued . . .

I love you, too!

J.P. Fitzgerald hung up his cell phone. "Damn," he said, his eyes locked on the cover of Mikhail Lermontov's *A Hero of Our Time.* He'd been reading it since he and Hana arrived at McMaster University, deciding, as they were driving along Forsyth Avenue a while ago, to park the car, drop a blanket down on the lawn outside Wentworth House and let Hana's five-year-old son, Wesley, play on the nearby daycare playground.

"One of your clients?" Hana asked, her eyes on Wesley, who was now trying to climb up the front of the slide.

J.P. nodded. "Yeah."

"Difficult case?"

J.P. shrugged, "Don't know, actually. I haven't completely figured her out yet."

"Really?" Hana asked, taking her eyes off Wesley and looking at J.P., surprised by what he'd just said.

"Well, she's not your average addict."

"How so?"

"Her rationale is . . . I don't know, it's very convincing."

"What's her rationale?"

"She claims she's a philanthropist."

"And she's not?"

"Well, that's just it. In a manner of speaking, I suppose she is."

Hana waited for J.P. to continue and when he didn't she smiled and said, "If you don't want to talk about it, I'll understand."

J.P. sat there for a moment, debating whether or not to tell her. Despite the fact that Hana was a psychologist, he rarely discussed his clients with her.

"Have you ever heard of Cesare Beccaria?" he asked, after a few more moments.

Hana shook her head.

"Well, Cesare Beccaria wrote this essay almost 250 years ago, around 1760, called 'On Crimes and Punishments' and in the essay he stated that humans are basically motivated by pleasure and pain and that if we don't have something, whether it's food or shelter or love or money or peace or education or the opportunity to be heard, then chances are we're in pain and so the most rational thing we can do is to try and get rid of the pain, which, sometimes, involves committing a crime. And so, Beccaria concluded that if we really want to reduce or get rid of crime, we have to make it a less rational response."

"That makes sense."

"Sure it does. Unfortunately for my client there is no Beccarianist clause in our legal system that makes an exception for those persons stealing from the haves and giving to the have-nots in order to ease their pain and create a more just society."

"So your client is really a thief, then?"

"Well, yeah. But she doesn't see herself as a thief. She considers herself a philanthropist and uses Cesare Beccaria as her rationale which, like you said, makes sense."

Hana smiled. "She sounds fascinating."

J.P. nodded. "Yeah, she's quite a piece of work."

"Well, if she's so convinced she's doing the right thing, why did she hire you?"

"She didn't. Her husband did."

"She's married?"

"For eighteen years."

"You're joking, right?"

"Nope. Married, mother of three, works part time at a health club."

"So, I take it she wants to see you?"

J.P. nodded.

"Where is she?"

"The Bean Bar."

"Well, at least she's close by."

J.P. sighed, nodding his head. "I was hoping to finish this today," he said, picking up his book.

Eight years ago, after dropping out of university, he went to the campus bookstore and bought a knapsack full of books, mostly novels, and started reading a book every couple of weeks, beginning his education in earnest. In March of this year he started reading the Russians — Tolstoy, Chekhov, Dostoevsky — and, although he was in awe of Tolstoy's and Dostoevsky's descriptive powers, and Chekhov's writing style, he felt that Lermontov, the young man who inspired all three of these great writers, was the only one worthy of his unadulterated admiration. In fact, J.P. so completely identified with Pechorin, the protagonist of *A Hero of Our Time*, that he felt a kinship with him across time and space, an *esprit de corps* that was left undiminished by the fact that Pechorin was merely a character conjured from Lermontov's imagination nearly two hundred years ago in Russia.

"Are you enjoying it?" Hana asked, pointing to the book.

J.P. nodded. "A lot. Did you know that Lermontov was only twenty-four or twenty-five when he wrote this?"

"Wow. That's amazing."

"It makes me envious."

"Why?"

"Because I'm almost thirty and I haven't even come close to doing something like this."

"What about your business?" Hana said, looking over the rim of her sunglasses, her eyes surveying J.P.'s sprinkling of chest hair; the residue of winter fat coating his stomach muscles; the scar on his left leg just above the knee from falling on a portage during a three-week canoe trip in Algonquin Park when he was a teenager.

"My business?" J.P. said, setting his book aside before standing up and pulling on his white tank top. "I don't see the correlation between writing a book that's been in print for over two hundred years and my business."

"Well, I do. You're attending to the needs of our time. Like your business card says, you provide viable solutions to postmodern-day dilemmas."

"Yeah, I know, but —"

"J.P., we both know you're so far ahead of today's psychiatry, it's not even funny. I mean, the things they're teaching in universities and hospitals nowadays are totally outdated. Most psychologists or psychiatrists don't have a clue as to why people are walking around feeling the way they do, why they have these enormous mood swings, why they feel empty or emotionless or full of rage, let alone where all these bizarre addictions and behaviours come from. But you, you're not only able to understand the why, you're also able to get them to recognize the source of their problems. You're able to show them what's going on, you're able to help them — and you do it without prescribing them a single drug."

J.P. shrugged. "Yeah, but I —"

"Look at what you did for Claudia."

"Who?"

"Claudia DeAngelo, my old classmate. You met her last week at my university reunion. She was talking to you about her boyfriend, Phillip, remember? The guy having all the problems? You gave her your business card."

"Oh yeah, right."

"Did you see how excited she was? She thought you could really help Phillip."

J.P. smiled. "I'm not so sure her boyfriend was the one who needed the help."

"So? She was so relieved just to talk to someone who understood what her boyfriend was experiencing. Who knows, someday someone may write about you and two hundred years from now people will be talking about J.P. Fitzgerald — a hero of our time."

J.P. laughed, beginning to button up his blue, short-sleeved Calvin

Klein collared shirt, and then, after doing up the last button, he bent over and kissed Hana on the cheek. "You're a good woman, Hana."

"Thanks," she replied, smiling. "You taking the car?"

J.P. shook his head. "It's only a ten-minute walk from here."

"How long do you think you'll be?"

"I don't know — an hour, maybe two."

"Do you want me to pick you up?"

"No, that's okay. I'll just meet you guys back at the apartment."

"Want me to make us some dinner?"

"If you feel up to it."

"Pad Thai sound okay to you?"

"Sounds amazing. I'll grab a bottle of wine on my way back."

"Perfect."

"Okay," J.P. said, bending over and giving her a long kiss. "I'll see you in an hour or two."

"Call if you're going to be longer, okay?" Hana said, pulling him down for another kiss.

"I will," J.P. said, kissing her, and then, after running over to Wesley and giving him a big bear hug, he ran back to Hana, gave her another quick kiss, then hopped the fence enclosing the playground and started jogging in the direction of Sterling Avenue.

"I love you!" Hana called after him.

"I love you, too!" a young woman shouted back from the open window of a silver Porsche 911 Carrera.

To Be Continued . . .

I hate you, too!

"Keira!"

"What?"

"You shouldn't do things like that."

"Why?"

"You never know how people are going to react."

"Oh come on, Dad. It was totally harmless. I highly doubt the guy's going to gun me down for saying 'I love you' to his girlfriend."

"You never know."

Keira, now glaring at her father, thought about suggesting that the real reason he didn't want her shouting such things from his car window was because he was afraid of someone keying his Porsche, a gift to himself after divorcing his second wife — Keira's mother.

"You know, Dad, you might be just a tad paranoid."

"I'm practical, not paranoid. And didn't I ask you to stop calling me Dad?"

"Why?"

"Because it makes me feel old."

"You *are* old, Dad."

"I'll bet you I'm the youngest looking forty-nine-year-old you know," her father said, looking at himself in the rear-view mirror. "People tell me I look thirty-five all the time."

Ya, maybe to your face, Keira said to herself, giving her father a once over. Behind your back they're probably saying if you didn't have regular Botox injections, a hair transplant, a spray-on tan, and a personal trainer, you'd look sixty.

"So," Keira said, scrutinizing her father's restructured hairline, which, she had to admit, did look pretty good, "we should probably hurry up so we don't miss the start of the movie."

"Actually, I think I might have to pass on the movie," her father replied, glancing at his watch. "Something's come up."

"How original," Keira said, sighing.

Ever since he divorced Keira's mother a couple of years ago, her father had promised to spend one Saturday a month with Keira, doing whatever she wanted. However, as Keira had come to expect, instead of the two of them going for a walk and having a picnic at Webster's Falls, as she'd suggested when he called yesterday, her father had 'surprised' her by booking a workout for them at McMaster University with his personal trainer, Tara-Lyn, then a facial and a pedicure at Lubamera Spa and now, despite Keira's request to see a matinee before having dinner at The Mandarin, something — surprise, surprise — had come up, the something probably being an available tee-time at Glen Abbey Golf Club with some of his business associates.

"Anyway," her father said, ignoring her comment, "what were we talking about before?"

"Before what?"

"Before you yelled out the window at a complete stranger."

Keira shrugged her shoulders. "I forget," she said, wanting to see if he could remember without her prompting him.

It was less than a minute ago, you moron, Keira thought, shaking her head. She couldn't believe his lack of interest in her life, how easily she slipped his mind. It wasn't that long ago that she was 'Daddy's Precious Little Girl' and his number one priority. Nowadays, however, she was pretty sure she wasn't even in his top ten.

"Kyle!" her father said triumphantly, looking as though he'd just correctly answered the Daily Double in *Jeopardy*. "We were talking about Kyle. You were going to tell me what you've heard."

Kyle was her half-brother, her father's son from his first marriage. His first wife had Kyle when she was only twenty-one. Eighteen months later she died in a car crash after being struck by a car running a stop sign. Kyle was the only thing Keira's father had left from his first marriage, and all he seemed to want to talk about whenever he and Keira got together.

"Why do we always have to talk about Kyle?" Keira said, folding her arms across her chest. "I thought this was supposed to be *our* time together? Those were *your* words you know, Dad."

"Okay, well, why don't you tell me some more about you then?"

"For instance?"

"For instance, are you . . . are you smitten with anyone?"

"God no."

"No boyfriends?"

"None," Keira said, shaking her head, momentarily considering adding, 'For God's sake, look at my role model.'

"What about what's-his-name?"

"Who?"

"You know, that guy from, from . . . he was . . ."

Keira waited, once again not wanting to assist her father, enjoying watching him stammer and struggle to complete his sentence.

"He was, you know. Come on, Keira, help me out here — the guy whose father did the, you know . . ."

"No idea who you're talking —"

"Hey asshole!" her father shouted suddenly, interrupting her, blaring his horn at a yellow Volkswagen Golf crossing the intersection. "That's a stop sign you just drove through! Jerk!"

"Relax Dad," Keira said, noticing that her father's shouting had attracted the attention of several people walking along Sterling Avenue.

"How can I relax when assholes like that have a licence?" her father shouted out the driver's side window. "He's lucky he didn't kill someone."

"It's not that big a deal," Keira said, regretting the words as soon as they left her mouth, knowing almost word for word what her father would say.

"Not that big a deal? It's because of jerks like him that my first wife is dead. If that stupid idiot hadn't blown that stop sign she'd still be alive today and Kyle wouldn't have run off and quit his —"

"Dad, I don't mean to be rude but I know what happened. I've heard the story like a gazillion times. Besides, the guy got charged with reckless driving."

"Reckless driving. My wife dies and all that asshole got was a ticket."

"Dad, maybe you should —"

"Listen, Keira, are you going to tell me what you know about Kyle?"

Keira repositioned her crossed arms. "I take it we're done talking about me, then?"

"Keira, I'm in no mood right now."

She sighed. "I really like this street. It reminds me of —"

"Keira."

"I don't know what to tell you, Dad."

"I just want to know what he's up to these days."

"I already told you before, I have no idea."

"Keira," her father said, his voice louder, more stern. "I know you know something."

Her father was right. She did know something. Much more than something, actually. She'd received dozens of e-mails from Kyle over the past couple of months. He'd been travelling around North America after quitting his job, the one her father had gotten him at some tech firm in Silicon Valley. Kyle had been her father's protégé and it nearly destroyed him when he found out that Kyle had quit and taken off without telling anyone. Her father was desperate for an explanation.

"Can we stop for a frozen yogurt?" Keira said, motioning to TCBY as her father slowed the Porsche, approaching the intersection at King and Sterling.

"Isn't yogurt fattening?" her father said, his tone indicting.

"They have fat-*free* yogurt there, Dad."

"Fat-free doesn't mean calorie-free, honey," he said, raising an eyebrow.

"Dad, take a look at me," Keira said, uncrossing her arms. "I'm like totally thin."

"You're not *that* thin," her father replied, gazing disapprovingly at her thighs.

"Oh my God, Dad. I'm like borderline anorexic."

He shrugged. "I don't know. You could probably stand to lose an inch or two off your thighs."

Keira growled. "Do you ever wonder how it made my mother feel to have you constantly bugging her to lose weight and then, practically the moment she fit into the size two dress you bought for her as motivation, she discovered you were having an affair with some woman twice the size of Monica Lewinsky?"

"Honey, I was merely pointing out that fat-free doesn't mean calorie-free and that maybe you —"

"Trust me, I know what you were doing," Keira replied, cutting her father short, and then, after a momentary pause, she said, "You know, Dad, in case you're interested, your little eyebrow raising and snide comments about my thighs makes me want to do the exact opposite of what you suggest."

"I thought you outgrew that last year."

"Outgrew what?"

"Doing the opposite of what I suggested."

"Dad, you know —"

"Okay, we'll go get a frozen yogurt."

"Really?"

Her father nodded. "But only if you tell me what you know about Kyle."

"Dad, that's blackmail."

"No, it's bribery. There's a difference."

"Whatever," Keira sighed, simultaneously thinking her father was a complete jerk and wondering, as she looked at the self-satisfied smug expression smeared on his face, how women could find him attractive, what her mother ever saw in him, why his new girlfriend, only three years older than Keira, would want to be with him. Sure, he was in good shape for his age, drove a nice car, and had lots of money, but he wasn't a particularly attractive man. She just couldn't imagine how any woman — no matter what the age — could look at him and think this is the man I want to marry. Or sleep with. Gross.

"Well, what's it going to be?" her father asked, drumming his fingers impatiently on the console.

"Okay, fine. I'll tell you."

"Thank you," her father said, making a left and pulling into a parking space beside Cottage Florists.

"Well?"

"Can't we talk about this over a yogurt?"

Her father shook his head. "The information first," he said, locking the power doors.

"You know, Dad, I don't think you'd understand."

Her father laughed. "Try me."

"Okay, well, all I can tell you is that he's in Ottawa right now and plans on staying there for the rest of the summer. Maybe longer."

"Ottawa? What's he doing there?"

"He didn't say."

"Does he at least have a job?"

Keira shrugged. "I don't know."

"Did he tell you why he quit his old job?"

Keira shook her head.

"That's it? That's all you know?"

Keira nodded. "Can we go to TCBY now?"

Her father pounded the steering wheel. "I know there's more to it than just this. I know for a fact he would've never done this without being influenced and if I ever catch the bastard responsible for corrupting my son I'll —"

"Dad, I don't think he was corrupted."

"You don't call ditching a $150,000 a year job with full benefits and a company car corrupted? I swear, if I ever hear who did it, I'll kill him."

"Dad, can we please go to TCBY now?"

Her father glanced at his watch. "Tell you what, sweetie," he said, reaching into his pocket and pulling out a few twenty-dollar bills. "Why don't you take this and buy yourself whatever you want — just make sure it's low-fat — and then take a taxi home. Okay?"

Keira rolled her eyes and groaned. "Typical," she murmured.

"What was that?"

She snatched the money out of her father's hand. "Nothing. Are you going to let me out?" she asked, her hand on the car door handle.

"Not before I get a hug and a kiss."

"Dad, do you realize that the only two ways you can get people to do things is through blackmail or bribery?"

"Whatever it takes to get a hug from Daddy's Precious Little Girl. Now come here," he said, reaching for her.

Keira hugged him quickly and got out of the car.

"You know, I sometimes wonder what you'd be like if you didn't have the luxury of money to make up for your other faults," she said.

Her father smiled, revved the engine, then tooted the horn twice and sped off, shouting, "I love you!"

"I hate you!" she called after him, giving him the finger.

"I hate you, too!" replied a man on the other side of the street in front of Ted Hendry's No Mean Feat.

It was the same man she'd seen hop the playground fence in McMaster University a few minutes ago, the one whose girlfriend she'd yelled back to.

Keira smiled. "Touché," she said, loud enough for the man to hear.

The man smiled and continued walking along King Street.

Turning in the direction of TCBY, Keira hesitated, mentally conjuring an image of the size two little black dress in her closet that her father had bought for her sixteenth birthday, writing, in the accompanying card, that if she could always fit into this dress she'd never have to worry about being single. After subtracting the amount of calories contained in a frozen yogurt from how many calories she'd burned during her workout at the university and realizing she had over a hundred calories to spare, she walked to TCBY and ordered a blueberry frozen yogurt before seating herself on the patio, taking out her cell phone and calling her brother.

To Be Continued . . .

218 days off

"Keira? Keira, slow down . . . Slow. Down . . . Thank you. Okay, listen. For one thing, I've never asked you to cover for me. Go ahead, tell Dad. I don't care . . . No, I don't. *You're* the one who cares. I stopped caring about what he thought a long time ago . . . Listen, I'm talking to someone right now . . . Yes, that's right, another convert. Ha. Ha. Gotta go. I'll call you back . . . Yes, I will. I don't know, maybe ten minutes or so, okay? . . . Okay. Talk to you soon. Bye."

Kyle hung up the phone. "Sorry about that," he said, turning around to face the man he'd been talking to. "Where was I?"

"You were talking about decreased attention spans," the man said, smiling at Kyle.

"Right. Thank you," Kyle said, giving himself an imaginary pat on the back. He'd chosen his mark well. The key, of course, is to know your target audience. He'd been strolling through Jackson Square for almost two hours with minimal success before spotting this particular man browsing the Self-Help section in Coles bookstore. Five minutes later they were walking through Gore Park, en route to the parking lot where the man had parked his car.

"The average person's attention span these days is appalling," Kyle said, making a slight detour to drop a loonie into the outstretched hand of a young homeless girl propped up against the edge of the Park fountain. "I mean, nowadays, we're not interested in listening to something longer than a thirty-second commercial or reading something longer than a Nike ad."

The man chuckled.

"This, of course," Kyle said, "is in stark contrast to fifty or sixty years ago when people used to sit for three, four, sometimes six hours at a time, listening to someone like Winston Churchill speak."

"Well, I certainly don't have six hours."

"How about six minutes?"

The man looked at his watch. "I've barely got that."

"I'll be quick."

"Tell you what, I'll give you until we get to my car."

"Deal. I'll need to give you some of my background first, if you don't mind."

"It's your story," the man replied, increasing his pace slightly.

"Okay, well, up until a while ago I worked for a fairly large U.S.-based firm. Since they were in the tech business, the products and technology they used were routinely being upgraded, which, of course, required us, the employees, to consistently update our skills. Anyway, after a few years of working there, I started to feel like Sisyphus. You ever heard of Sisyphus?"

The man shook his head.

"Well, Sisyphus is the guy from Greek mythology condemned to push a massive rock up a hill only to have it roll back down again once he reaches the top. And this was how I felt about the job I was doing. I mean, every time I thought I had a handle on things, another upgrade in technology would occur and I'd have to once again spend some more time learning the new programs. Of course, even though having to learn all this new stuff and do all this extra work every few weeks was stressing me out, I still kept doing it. And the reason I kept doing it was because I actually thought there was something wrong with me. I mean, I'd take a look around me and see other people in my firm doing the extra work necessary to keep up and not complaining about it and so I thought the reason I was feeling so stressed out and anxious was because there was some problem or fault I had."

Kyle looked at the man. "Still with me?"

"So far so good," the man replied, stepping around a crowd of people lined up at the Upper Wellington bus stop.

"Great. So, anyway, I guess I'd been working for the firm for almost four years when I met this guy who totally changed my life. I was in Toronto for a conference and I was on my way back to my hotel when I heard some guy on the street corner ranting about how ludicrous our economic system is. I don't know why, but, instead of ignoring him like everyone else was, I decided to stop and listen to him and a few minutes later I was telling him about my job and how the firm I was working for was constantly pushing its employees to become more and more efficient and how this was creating tons of stress for me. As I was telling him this, the guy started smiling and shaking his head and told me that my experience reminded him of what Loren Pierce Coleman said about how our society's definition of efficiency comes from the efficiency of a machine, which really isn't such a good definition for people, because, like this guy said, it's not like these machines are sitting there thinking they want to spend more time painting or reading or meditating or playing music or visiting their neighbours or how crummy it feels to not have dinner with their family for the third night in a row because they've got to learn some new computer software program. And it was at that particular moment that I realized what I'd been trying to do all this time — I was trying to become more like the technology I was using."

At this point, Kyle paused, giving the man an inquiring look. "You wouldn't happen to be a Trekkie, by any chance, would you?"

"A what?"

"A fan of *Star Trek*. You know, a Trekkie."

"I've seen a few episodes."

"So you know who Data is, then?"

The man nodded.

"And so you know that Data is an android who is always trying to be more human, right?"

Again, the man nodded.

"Well, while talking to this guy I realized I was the opposite of Data. I was a human being who was trying to be more like a machine.

And so I realized, I mean, *really* realized, how insane this was and how I needed to do other things because not only was I spending far too much time either at work or thinking about work, but this particular vision of efficiency was driving me insane."

"So I take it you quit?" the man said, smiling as he turned up John Street.

"Well, not right away. What I actually did was I went into work the following week and reviewed the amount of work I'd done for the firm during my second year there — which was the year I received my first *productivity* award — and then for the next few weeks I did *that* amount of work. And what I discovered was that with the *aid* of the new computers and new software programs and the other available tech support, I could usually finish my work a lot sooner and so what I decided to do instead of staying and doing more work was leave."

"What do you mean?"

"What I mean is as soon as I was finished doing a certain amount of work I'd leave, whether it was after being there for six hours or only three hours."

The man started chuckling.

"What's so funny?" Kyle asked.

"I can see where this is headed," the man said, a bemused expression on his face. "You got fired, right?"

Kyle smiled. "After a few weeks of working like this one of the firm's managers called me into his office and asked me what the heck I was doing and after I explained to him that I was doing exactly the same amount of work as I'd done when I received a slew of excellent evaluations and my first productivity award, the manager told me that times had changed, that the firm had a responsibility to their shareholders to remain competitive and in order to do that, the *old* level of productivity wasn't acceptable anymore. Of course, when I decided to continue working at the *old* level I ended up — as you already guessed — getting fired. And I sued them."

"Did you win?"

"We settled out of court."

"Satisfactory result?"

"Half a year's salary."

"Not bad. And then what?"

"Well, using the money I got from the settlement, I started travelling all over North America and talking about what happened to me to anyone who would listen. I've spent the past few months going from city to city telling people how this so-called efficient way of working *militates* against the essence of humanity, how it actually goes against the U.S. constitution and Article 3 and 4 of the UN Charter of Rights and Article 23-1 of the Universal Declaration of Human Rights. When I was in the U.S., I'd tell people things like if this was the 'land of the free' we wouldn't be enslaved to The Company, or if this was 'the home of the brave' we wouldn't be totally afraid to say anything *against* The Company for fear of being reported, written up, reviewed, downsized, or fired. Or if we had the right to life, liberty, and the pursuit of happiness then we'd be getting technology to work for us instead of working for technology."

"You know something," the man said, looking directly at Kyle for the first time since they'd left Jackson Square. "That's some interesting stuff."

"Yeah, well," Kyle said, motioning to the man that the light had changed and they could begin walking across Main Street, "I'd love to take credit for it, but I'm basically regurgitating what the guy I met in Toronto told me."

The man chuckled. "I'm starting to see why you decided to stop and listen to him."

Kyle nodded. "Yeah. He was pretty persuasive. And inspiring. I mean, the guy was full of info. For instance, did you know that in 1967 the *New York Times* predicted that 'in the year 2000, people will work no more than four days a week and less than eight hours a day' and that if you included 'legal holidays and long vacations this could result in an annual working period of only 147 days with 218 days off'?"

"Really?"

"Yep. It used to be that *reducing* the number of hours a person worked was the definition of success, that was how you determined how *profitable* or how *successful* your company or your country was."

"Well, that definition has certainly changed," the man said.

"I know. Now it's all about productivity and efficiency!" Kyle said. "And *that's* what I'm concerned about. I'm concerned about what this change in the definition of economic success is actually doing to people. What effect it has on them. And, I mean, when you realize that three of the most prescribed drugs in the U.S. are an ulcer medication, a hypertension reliever, and a tranquillizer, it doesn't exactly take a genius to figure out that this so-called *efficient* way of working isn't really working."

The man laughed.

"What?"

"I'm just thinking of a few of my colleagues, not to mention my wife, and their so-called prescriptions."

Kyle nodded. "I know, it's crazy, isn't it? But it's also why whenever I'm talking to people about this sort of thing almost everyone feels the same way. And the thing that I always find interesting is how most of these people think they're the *only* ones who feel like this. Which is probably why, just like I was, they're afraid to say something. In the last few months, I've had literally hundreds of people tell me they knew something was wrong — really wrong — to the point where every cell in their body was screaming that things shouldn't be this way, that they shouldn't be working like this."

"And so what do you tell people to do?"

"The same thing the guy in Toronto told me to do — encourage people to stop rushing to escape or deny or ignore or *fix* these kinds of feelings and intuitions. That, instead, they should be listening to them, trusting them, and acting on them. And it's also why every chance I get I urge people to . . . oh, hang on, I can feel my cell phone vibrating. It's probably just my sister again. Just a second."

Kyle hit the TALK button on his cell phone. "I thought I said I was going to call *you* back, Keira?"

To Be Continued . . .

"Yeah, in ten minutes. It's been exactly twelve minutes and thirty-seven seconds . . . I don't need to relax. *You* need to keep your promises . . . Kyle, I'm coming very close to having a meltdown here . . . At the TCBY in Westdale . . . That's too long . . . *Still* too long . . . That's the best you can do? . . . Okay. I'll be waiting."

Keira sighed, hung up her cell phone and made two more calls — one to her mother, who wasn't home, and one to her third best friend, Becky, who was in a fitting room in Tommy Hilfiger in Limeridge Mall trying on a pair of jeans and asked Keira to come and meet her there, which at first seemed like a good idea, but then, after Keira realized she'd have to go home first, have a shower, do her hair, put on make-up and one of her new outfits since she was severely underdressed for going shopping with Becky, she said she was too tired.

"I'm pretty beat from my workout so I think I'll just go home and flake out on the couch for a while. But give me a call when you're done shopping."

"Will do," Becky said. "Peace out."

"See ya," Keira replied before hanging up and heaving a long, loud sigh.

Could I be any more bored? Keira said to herself, setting her cell phone down on the patio table. For a moment, she thought about getting another frozen yogurt, and then her father's words and incriminating glance at her thighs popped into her head and she decided against it, turning her attention instead to a group of girls, probably no more than six or seven years old, giggling and squealing and playing tag in the parking lot in front of Walker's Chocolates.

What I wouldn't give to be their age again, Keira mused. Life would be so much simpler. I wouldn't have to deal with the fact that my father is an adulterer and a liar; that my mother is on Prozac and prays every night for my father to come home; that my step-brother was so disillusioned with capitalism that he quit a high-paying job to wander around North America preaching to people in hopes of changing our current economic system; that the guy I was dating last month dumped me for another guy, telling me he'd always been somewhat bi-curious. "What the hell am I going to do?" she said, aloud, sighing.

"You could get pregnant again."

The comment came from one of the two women standing at the corner of Newton Avenue and King Street, waiting for the light to change.

"Pregnant?" the taller woman replied, giving the shorter woman a look as though she were certifiably psychotic. "Are you kidding? I'll never do that again. Never. I hated the way my body looked."

"Really?"

"Absolutely hated it."

"Why?"

"It just wasn't me. I'd look in the mirror and I'd see this completely different person reflected back to me."

"Really? I loved the way I looked. I loved being pregnant. It was the best time of my life. Everyone was so kind to me."

"I loathed every single second of it. The morning sickness, the backaches, the unwanted attention. It was like people suddenly felt they had the right to touch me, to rub my stomach. I had complete strangers touching me."

"I loved that."

"Even worse were the stretch marks."

Her friend laughed. "I call them 'beauty marks.'"

"Beauty marks? What's so beautiful about having permanent gashes across your stomach and breasts? I have to wear a one-piece bathing suit for the rest of my life."

"I still wear a two-piece."

"Well, you're braver than I am."

When the light changed and the women began crossing the street, Keira felt an urge to call out to them, to ask them to come back and have a seat on the patio and continue their conversation.

"Where are we going, Grandpa?"

Turning in the direction of the voice, Keira saw an elderly man and a young girl walking along Newton Avenue, approaching King Street.

"To the forest, Miss Katie. The forest."

"Shouldn't I change first?" the young girl asked as they walked past Keira.

After quickly surveying the young girl's floral-patterned yellow sundress and black penny loafers, the elderly man shook his head. "You should be fine."

"Grandma's going to be mad if I get my dress dirty."

"Not to worry," the elderly man said, putting his hand on the young girl's shoulder. "You can use my jacket."

As the elderly man and his granddaughter crossed King Street, Keira was struck by all the clothes the man was wearing, wondering how he could be comfortable in his bulky barn jacket and overalls.

"I have no idea."

This voice came from a woman crossing Newton Avenue, walking towards Keira. She was talking to another, slightly heavier woman. Both of them were wearing exercise gear and carrying two Evian water bottles, one in each hand.

"Wait, are you talking about the billboards in the east end, near Stelco and Dofasco?"

"Not just there. They're all over the city. They have these giant black X's on them."

"Yeah, I've seen them. What do think it's all about?"

Keira smiled to herself. This is better than channel surfing, she thought, easing back into the patio chair. And everything's in 3-D.

"I think it's vandalism," one of the women said.

"Really?"

"I'll bet you it's just a bunch of teenagers going around defacing —"

The rest of the woman's sentence was drowned out by a large dump truck rumbling through the intersection. By the time it was far enough away to enable Keira to hear them again, the women were out of earshot, leaving a temporary vacuum of conversation until a young guy rounding the corner of TCBY with a frozen yogurt in his hand said, "I've got one," to the girl following him out onto the patio.

"Shoot," the girl said, plopping down at the table next to Keira, spooning a scoop of yogurt into her mouth.

"Okay, what are the Top Five things you would never do and your reason or reasons for not doing them?"

"Nice one," the girl replied. "Very nice."

"Well?"

"Well, I think you've probably got your top five already lined up so why don't you go first?"

"Okay. And, as always, these are in no particular order, but number one would have to be to never have more than two kids."

"Reason?"

"Well, you know how people like to complain about the population, saying that there's not enough resources to support the number of people on the earth, well, the truth is, it's not a population problem, it's a consumption problem. And, specifically a *North American* consumption problem. We feel all horrible about poor people in Africa and India and South America, telling each other we have to improve their basic needs and increase their standard of living when what we really should be doing is changing the so-called basic needs and the standard of living of the middle and upper classes in North America because we're the ones actually impoverishing the Earth and making people poor. I mean, when you consider that one person in North America consumes sixty times the amount of energy and resources of a person in India or one hundred times the amount of a person in Ethiopia, you begin to realize that the real problem has to do with consumption — and the source of the problem is right here in our own backyard."

"Number two?"

"Number two would be to never tell anyone but you how I feel about 9/11."

"Reason?"

"Well, since 9/11 most of the U.S. resources — financial, academic, physical, intellectual, even spiritual — are being diverted towards fighting terrorism, which means we have less resources to devote to much more destructive things. I mean, sure, terrorism is pretty crappy, but it causes only a fraction of deaths when you compare it to things like heart disease, malnutrition, car accidents, suicides, AIDS, and cancer. And, yeah, I realize it gives the U.S. something to do, but when there are all these other things that are far more lethal to humanity, you'd think they'd be directing their efforts and money towards these things."

"No argument there. Number three?"

"Number three would be eating a food or buying something that I didn't know what it consisted of or where it came from."

"Reason?"

"I think there should be a mandatory Ingredient List for all products. Like every single product, whether it's a toy, a home, a shoe, a piano, a desk, a computer, or whatever should come with a Real Ingredient List attached to it that states in precise detail what the product contains. And by contains I don't just mean things like the raw materials, I also mean things like, 'How far did it have to travel to get to this shelf? How many resources were used? What was the motivation for making this product? Was it profit, prestige, celebrity? Was the product made with child labour? Was it made out of fear, resentment, hostility? Was something or someone exploited, isolated, harmed, contaminated, or destroyed as a result of the product being manufactured?' And the reason for all this information being provided for the consumer is because all this is actually contained in the product and potential consumers need to know this because when their children play with a toy or they wear the shoes or eat the food or use the computer or live in the home, they'll be absorbing and becoming part of everything that went into making it."

"Well, I can see someone's given this particular Top Five question some serious thought, huh? Number four?"

"Number four would be saying, 'I'm bored.'"

"Reason?"

"Because there are so many things you could be doing. I mean, George Steiner said something about how all the great wars and inventions and events have already occurred and people are being left with this feeling of being pensioned before their first battle, but I think he's wrong. I mean, there are literally hundreds of battles you could be involved in these days. There is so much injustice out there. You could spend years battling for women's rights or native rights or preventing species extinction or the logging of old growth forests or cultural genocide or a whole slew of other things."

"And — ladies and gentlemen, may I have your attention, please — number five?"

"Number five would have to be . . . tell you what. Let's go back to the house and while we're walking I'll tell you number five, okay?"

"Sounds good. Wanna make the light?"

"Let's go!"

When Keira turned to watch them running across King Street, she noticed a man standing in front of The Adventure Attic, waving at her. Dressed in a beige short-sleeved collared shirt, cargo shorts, and hiking boots, he was carrying a small book in his non-waving hand. After looking behind and beside her on both sides and seeing no one else returning his wave, Keira hesitantly waved, causing the man to smile and Keira to wonder who the heck he thought she was.

When the light changed, the man started walking towards her, still smiling. As he drew nearer, however, Keira noticed his facial expression quickly changing from an 'I'm-so-happy-to-see-you' expression to confusion to disappointment to embarrassment and then to something resembling an 'I'm-just-going-to-pretend-to-be-interested-in-something-behind-you-to-make-it-seem-like-you-were-imagining-the-whole-thing' before he walked past her without saying a word.

"Jerk," Keira said, nearly under her breath.

"I probably deserved that."

"Oh, I didn't realize . . ." Keira said, turning to see that the man had stopped walking and was now standing only a few feet from her. "I wasn't . . . I mean, I'm sorry."

"No. I'm the one who's sorry. It was my fault. I thought you were someone else. In fact, you look a lot like someone I just met a while ago — in that bookstore over there," he said, pointing at Bryan Prince Bookseller across the street. "You could be her twin."

"Is she meeting you here?"

"No. I just thought — hoped, actually — that you were her."

"So, you came back just to see if she was still around?"

"Well, no, not really. Of course, that would've been nice. However, I was actually on my way to pay for this book."

The man held up the book and Keira read the title, *"Surfacing,"* aloud, before asking, "You mean you stole it?"

The man laughed, shaking his head. "I forgot to pay for it."

"I take it you were quite smitten with this woman?"

The man chuckled.

"What's so funny?"

"The word, 'smitten.' I haven't heard someone use that word in years."

"My father uses it all the time," Keira said. "He gets 'smitten' with a different woman every other month."

"I take it that's not a good thing."

"Not if you're his daughter."

"Right. My name's Keith, by the way."

"Keira."

"Nice to meet you, Keira."

"You too, Keith."

"Well, I guess I should probably find out if the bookstore has put out an All Points Bulletin for my arrest."

"If you need a character witness, I'll vouch for you."

"Thanks. I may need it."

"And good luck with finding the woman."

Keith smiled. "Cheers."

"See ya," Keira said, watching him walk across the street and enter the bookstore.

A minute later, after eavesdropping on a couple of partial conversations, Keira saw Keith walking out of the bookstore. Just before he rounded the corner in front of The Adventure Attic he held the book up and shouted, "I got off with a slap on the wrist."

"I'd like to slap more than that."

The comment came from one of the two attractive Spanish-looking guys standing next to Keira's table. They were both gawking at Keith as he continued walking up Sterling Avenue.

"Is he a friend of yours?" the older of the two men asked Keira.

"Actually no, I just met him," she replied, returning Keith's goodbye wave.

"Was he trying to pick you up?"

Keira shook her head. "He thought I was someone else."

"Really? And what was your read on him, sweetie?"

"Excuse me?" Keira replied, somewhat confused.

"Sweetie, was he gay or straight?"

"Oh. Most definitely gay."

"I knew it!" the younger man squealed. "I should've gone out and made a scene."

"You're making one right now," the older man said, gesturing to the other patrons.

The younger man smiled. "Go back to your conversations, ladies and gentlemen. Nothing to hear — oh my God, Renaldo. Do *you* see what *I* see?" he said, gasping and pointing excitedly in the direction of the street, causing every head on the patio to turn in time to see two male cyclists making a right onto Sterling Avenue.

To Be Continued . . .

nothing R-rated

"Did you see the looks on their faces?" Tim asked, glancing back at the people seated on the patio outside TCBY.

"They probably think you're a professional cyclist," Ken said, nodding at Tim's cycling gear and the new Trek Cyclocross bike he bought the week before.

"Either that or they've never seen a guy my age riding a bike like this," Tim said, chuckling.

"Speaking of riding bikes, did you have any luck with your students this year?"

Tim shook his head. "Only two of them. But they don't need the exercise. They're already in great shape."

"Isn't that always the case?"

Tim nodded. "It's depressing. I can't believe how many overweight and out of shape kids there are at my school. We never had that when I was in school. I mean, sure, there was the odd one. But now it's as though two out of every three kids are supersized."

"I know what you mean," Ken said, slowing down for the stop sign at Haddon Avenue. "I walk around our neighbourhood in Toronto and see six-year-old boys with burger bellies and bitch tits lounging around the perimeter of basketball courts and soccer fields, inhaling bags of chips and pop and playing Gameboys."

"Oh, man, don't even get me started on video games. Every kid's a *virtual* football, basketball, or hockey player nowadays. The only thing that gets a real workout anymore are their thumbs."

Ken laughed. "My students think I'm a total geek because I don't know how to play video games. I tell them I never learned how to play that way and that I get far more enjoyment out of actually playing basketball or hockey than pretending to play it."

"They still slated to get rid of physical education classes in your school next year?"

"Yep."

"Ours too. I think it's criminally negligent. We have a responsibility to these kids to keep them physically healthy and here we are, abandoning the only class that can do that for them."

"I know, it's crazy," Ken said, nodding. "With the one hand we're tossing out physical education and with the other we're giving the thumbs up to having more and more greasy, sugary, nutritionally bankrupt junk food in our cafeterias. It's like the kids don't have a chance."

"You'd almost think we're intentionally fattening them."

Ken chuckled. "Who knows, maybe it's some big experiment to see how many obese, diabetic teenagers we can have by the year 2020 or something."

Tim shook his head. "You know what I'd like to see?"

"What?"

"People start to sue the crap out of the fast food industry the same way they did the tobacco industry."

"Haven't a few people already tried that?"

"Yeah, but I mean everyone."

"You really think that's a good idea?"

"Sure, why not? The companies know what's in the food they make. They know what this does to a person's health. And they still continue to sell it."

"True. But people also have to learn to regulate themselves. I mean, this way, every fat bastard in the country who hasn't an ounce of restraint is going to blame it on McDonald's. I can just see them all lined up in our courtrooms wearing little T-shirts that say, 'McDonald's Made Me Do It.'"

Tim laughed. "Yeah, you're right. I guess what I'm trying to say is that, to some extent, someone or something is to blame."

"I know. But the problem is systemic. I mean, take a look at the way our cities are designed. Everything is geared towards making things easier for the automobile. Pedestrians aren't taken into consideration, other modes of transportation like skateboards, bicycles, and inline skates are an afterthought at best. All our subdivisions and retail outlets are designed to drive to. I mean, compare that to a place like Holland where you've —"

"Hey, you don't have to tell me about Holland."

"Oh yeah, that's right. I forgot. That's where you guys went for your honeymoon, right?"

Tim nodded. "A two-week bike tour," he replied, braking for the stop sign at Dalewood. While waiting for a car to go through the intersection, he pointed at the trees lining Sterling Avenue. "Every time I come down this street in the summer I feel like I'm cycling through a large leafy tunnel."

"Yeah, it's nice. Hey, is that McMaster University ahead of us?"

"Yep."

"That where we're headed?"

"Sort of."

A few moments later, after they paused at the stop sign near the entrance to McMaster's campus to admire the attractive young woman gathering up a blanket and talking with a young boy on the lawn outside the daycare playground, Tim motioned to Ken that they were turning right.

"Wow. Those houses over there are incredible," Ken said, moments later, pointing at the homes along Mayfair Crescent.

Tim nodded. "Yeah, they're pretty nice," he said, and then, pointing to a group of homes further along, he added, "The ones over there back onto a huge ravine. Really picturesque. Great trail riding, too."

"Is that a hint?"

"Feel up to it?"

"It's why we got these bikes, isn't it?" Ken said.

"You want to lead?" Tim asked as they approached the opening to the trail.

"What kind of action are we looking at?"

"PG, maybe AA in some spots. Nothing R-rated, though. We've seen worse."

Ken smiled. "Okay, I'll take point."

"Oh yeah," Tim said, just as Ken entered the trail. "There's usually a few nasty blowdowns a little ways in so don't get too carried away with your speed."

"Now he tells me," Ken replied, chuckling as he continued down the trail, slowly at first — slow enough to have a look around, remarking on the beauty of the ravine, how nice it would be to own a home that had this as your backyard — until, after negotiating several fallen trees, he increased his speed for a dozen or so pedal strokes before suddenly applying his brakes, noticing the path ahead was split.

"Which way," he shouted over his shoulder at Tim, "right or left?"

"Straight."

"Grandpa," Katie said, giving her grandfather a playful shove. "If they went straight they'd go right into the creek."

To Be Continued . . .

into the side of the hill

Norman and Katie were lying on their stomachs behind a fallen tree on top of the ravine, periodically scanning the surrounding area with their binoculars.

"That's exactly where I want them to end up. They shouldn't be riding these trails with their fancy mountain bikes."

"They're not mountain bikes," Katie stated, matter-of-factly. "They're Cyclocross bikes."

"And what, do I dare ask, is a Cyclocross bike?" Norman asked, stealing a quick glance at the two cyclists before they disappeared down the South Shore Trail.

"It's a hybrid. Part road racing bike and part mountain bike."

"And how does my dearest granddaughter know this?"

"I'm your *only* granddaughter, Grandpa," Katie said. "And I know this because I walked past Pierek's Cycle yesterday and they had one hanging outside their store."

Norman smiled. "You're very observant, Miss Katie."

"Thank you."

"You'll make a great scientist one day. That is, when you're not too busy saving people's lives."

"I didn't say I saved her life, Grandpa."

"Well, from the sounds of things, it seems to me if you hadn't pulled Miss Natasha off her skateboard the motorcycle would've hit her, maybe even, well . . ."

"Maybe."

Norman smiled, admiring his granddaughter's humility. "And did Miss Natasha thank you for saving her?"

"No," Katie said, shaking her head, immediately recalling Natasha yelling at her, insisting that she wasn't even close to the motorcycle, that now her elbow was bleeding and it was all Katie's fault. "She yelled at me and blamed me for scraping her elbow."

"Hmmm," Norman said, slowly tugging on his left eyebrow, "perhaps she was just embarrassed."

"Perhaps."

Norman watched Katie repositioning herself on his barn jacket before she once again looked through her binoculars. At times he couldn't believe how strong she was, how much she'd been able to endure these past few years. And then he'd remember she was his daughter's daughter.

"So, what did Miss Katie learn today?" Norman asked, giving her a pat on the back.

"I learned that an acre of hemp yields more than four times as much fibre as an acre of trees."

"Is that so?"

"Yes. And hemp actually helps clean the soil of chemicals while it grows."

"I never knew that."

"And you can harvest it two times a year, not like trees where once you cut them down you have to wait twenty-five or fifty years to get a good-sized tree again."

"Now that I *did* know."

"Well, did you know that hemp can be used to make all the same kinds of things trees are being used for, things like paper and rope and fibreglass and plywood and boxes?"

Norman nodded. "Up until World War Two they used hemp all the time. After the war the government didn't allow it anymore because it took money away from the forestry and pulp and paper industry."

Katie sighed. "Do you think we have to run out of trees before people realize what an amazing product hemp is, Grandpa?"

Norman chuckled. "Hopefully not, Miss Katie. Hopefully not," he said, picking up his binoculars and carefully scanning the far side of the ravine. "So, what else did you learn?" he asked a few moments later, his binoculars now on the small concrete bridge he'd walked over earlier in the day.

"I learned what the word irony means."

"You did. Give me an example of irony."

"Okay. It's ironic that the products we use to clean our homes are marked with skulls and crossbones and warnings about how toxic and poisonous they are."

"Very well done."

"How can people say a countertop or a bathtub is *clean* when the stuff they're using is toxic and poisonous? How can people think like that, Grandpa?"

Norman laughed. "Miss Katie, once again you pose a very good question. The answer to which will elude almost everyone who dares to ask it."

Katie smiled at her grandfather. She'd been accompanying him on hikes in Cootes Paradise since she was a baby. They'd spent countless days exploring the area together, figuring out the relationships between all the animals and trees and plants and soil and bacteria and the stream, discovering how they were all part of one related community, how everything fit together like a beautiful puzzle.

"By the way, how have you been sleeping lately?" Norman said, as if reading her thoughts.

Lately, she'd been bothered by a recurring dream. In the dream she's standing in the ravine and suddenly all the trees and insects and plants and animals and the stream itself start being cut and trampled and maimed and poisoned and destroyed and while this is happening, she doesn't move or speak or scream or try to stop it. And it isn't because she doesn't want to stop it, because she does, it's just that she doesn't know how to stop it. She feels powerless to prevent it. And that's when she usually wakes up.

"Okay, I guess," Katie replied.

"Still having bad dreams?"

Katie nodded.

"I did some research," Norman said, gently rubbing Katie's back, "and I discovered you're not alone."

"Really?"

"Not even close. Apparently this is quite a common thing."

"It is?"

Norman nodded. "There have been thousands, maybe even tens of thousands, of documented cases of people having nightmares about rainforests or rivers or animals being destroyed and they wake up feeling guilty or ashamed because of what we've done and are still doing to the Earth."

"Why are they having them?"

"Well, there are many theories, but the one that made the most sense to me — and to the people having the dreams — is that we're all pieces of the beautiful puzzle and when even one tiny piece is lost or hurt or destroyed, all the other pieces suffer. And so the nightmares are a reaction to the pain and death we've caused the other pieces, a reaction to us seeing them not as valuable or precious in their own right, but as things to be used, abused, discarded, forgotten, or destroyed. And as long as we do this we'll continue to have people feeling guilty and having nightmares."

"That makes sense."

Norman smiled. "I believe you've read *The Catcher in the Rye*?"

Katie nodded her head. It had been on her grandmother's 'Required Reading List' this past year.

"Well, do you remember the part in the book when Holden talks about all these kids running through the rye fields towards him, unaware that they're heading for a cliff and he's there to catch them before they fall off?"

Katie nodded.

"That's how I see you, only instead of protecting the kids like Holden did, you're protecting all the animals and plants and the other pieces of the puzzle."

Katie smiled. "I love you, Grandpa."

"I love you, too, Miss Katie," Norman said, planting a kiss on her cheek.

"That tickles," Katie said, giggling and rubbing her face where Norman's beard had brushed against her cheek.

"It's camouflage," Norman replied, massaging his beard.

Katie smiled again, admiring her grandfather's outfit, his overalls, T-shirt, and the barn jacket she was lying on, which he never washed, ever, a trick he'd learned from his grandmother, who told him never to wear cologne or deodorants or wash his clothes because it would warn the animals that something foreign was coming into the forest instead of just plain ol' Norman. It was also why Katie thought it odd that her grandfather didn't mind that she was wearing her new dress or the fact that she was wearing vanilla-scented perfume.

"So, Grandpa, are you going to tell me what we're looking for?"

"We, my dear, are looking for a very rare mammal."

"I thought we'd already seen all the mammals here?"

"I did too," Norman said, his eyes once again buried in the binoculars, scanning. "In fact, I thought this particular mammal was extinct in this region. But, I'm fairly certain I spotted one today on my regular walk."

"Really? What did it look like?"

"Like *that*," Norman whispered, pointing excitedly in the direction of his binoculars.

Katie immediately pointed her binoculars in a similar direction and saw a man walking over the small concrete bridge. He was wearing a beige short-sleeved collared shirt, cargo shorts, and hiking boots and was carrying a book. When he reached the fork in the path — where a person could either take the path leading to McMaster University or the one that continued on to the South Shore Trails — the man paused, his eyes surveying the surrounding area for a few seconds before he took a completely different path, heading northeast, moving deftly through the dense underbrush and hopping over the stream before beginning to scamper up the hillside.

Occasionally he stopped to listen, glancing furtively in all directions as though he sensed someone was watching him until, during one of his stops, just when Katie thought he was going to continue, the man reached down and opened what appeared to be a small hatch door and disappeared into the side of the hill.

. . . . **To Be Continued . . .**

there aren't too many women . . . . .

"Home Sweet Home," Keith said as he closed the hatch, breathing in the earthy smell of roots, soil, and decaying matter mingling with the raspberry-flavoured tea he'd made himself before heading back to Bryan Prince Bookseller to pay for his book.

He'd scouted the location of 'The Burrow,' as he now called it, for over a week, watching the flow of hikers through the area, tracking their movements, determining which areas were the least travelled, before finally deciding on a relatively secluded spot that not one person had ventured near.

Over the course of the next three weeks, mostly during the night, he'd dug an underground bunker into the hillside, dispersing the excess earth over a wide area of the forest floor, using wood pilfered from various construction sites and dumpsters to hold up the earth like a mining shaft.

Once he had the internal structure built, he'd set about furnishing his new home. 'The Burrow' now contained a single bed that doubled as a table and could be flipped up to give more room; a comfortable rocking chair and foot stool salvaged from the sidewalk of a Westdale resident; a small double cupboard where he kept a good stock of non-perishable items such as canned soup, canned vegetables, brown beans, bottled water, a tin of salted licorice, tea, sugar, several small canisters of Coleman propane, two flashlights, and a good supply of batteries; and a Coleman stove on which he heated tea and the occasional warm meal. 'The Burrow' was also equipped with three small air vents, one of which doubled as an opening for a small, handmade periscope used to survey his surroundings prior to exiting.

Keith smiled to himself while lighting the Coleman lantern hanging above the bed, imagining what his sister would think of him trading the small room in his friend's basement for a hole in the ground.

Of course, I'm certain I'm not the first person to live in this bush, Keith mused. Just that the last person to do so may have been one of the original settlers of Hamilton. And, contrary to what his sister knew, he did have an ace up his sleeve. Or, to be more accurate, a lottery ticket in his knapsack.

He pulled his knapsack towards him and retrieved the lottery ticket from a small, hidden pocket on the inside of the sack. It was the Super 7 ticket he'd purchased in Toronto last summer. He had until August 17th to claim the prize: $250,000.

Since last fall he'd been house hunting, consulting the real estate listings in the *Hamilton Spectator* on a near daily basis. In early May, however, he was set to make an offer on a house near Bayfront Park when the idea to build 'The Burrow' came to him. He thought it was ideal. He showered at McMaster University; did his laundry at The Camel on Emerson Street; shopped at The Barn or Fortinos; had a library card; worked part-time for Planit Green, a small landscaping business, which gave him more than enough money to pay for his food, batteries, and kerosene for his lantern; and spent the remainder of his time reading, exploring the woods, and making entries in his journal.

"Still," he said to himself, thinking of the woman he'd met at Bryan Prince Bookseller earlier in the day, the younger woman he'd just seen at TCBY, and his sister's comments about him not being an attractive catch because of his present circumstances, "there aren't too many women who would want to call this place home."

After lighting the Coleman stove, pouring some bottled water into a pot, and placing the pot on the stove, Keith grabbed hold of his handmade periscope and began surveying the area surrounding 'The Burrow.' As he was picking his way up the hillside a few minutes earlier, he'd had the feeling he was being watched. Initially, he'd dismissed it as the usual paranoia he felt whenever he was returning 'home.' But now, he wanted to be sure his feelings were incorrect. After panning slowly from west to north to east and seeing nothing of consequence, Keith was about to let go of the periscope when he suddenly spotted a familiar couple traipsing down the trail that led to McMaster University, their eyes peering back at him.

To Be Continued . . .

maybe we should

Well, now. Even *I* didn't expect this, Norman thought to himself, recalling his earlier conversation with the not-so-young man and his suspicions that the man was up to something.

He and Katie had lay in silent observation for almost five minutes before Norman suggested they make their way down the ravine and back home, telling Katie that her grandmother would be expecting them back soon.

"Oh my gosh, Grandpa," Katie said, excitedly, her eyes alternating between the trail in front of her and the spot on the hillside where the man had disappeared. "What are we going to do?"

"We'll study him," Norman replied, admiring the man's location for building his 'home,' thinking he couldn't have chosen a better spot. "Just like we study the other birds and insects and mammals here."

"But don't you think we should tell someone?" Katie asked, already on the small concrete bridge, waiting for Norman to catch up.

"Absolutely not," Norman said, his voice suddenly stern, gently taking hold of Katie's arm when he reached her. "We won't tell anyone except your grandmother. It'll be our little secret. If we start telling people, what do you think will happen?"

"He'll leave."

"Exactly," Norman said, releasing Katie's arm before crossing the bridge. "In a matter of days, everyone would be here."

"I guess you're right," Katie said, glancing one last time in the direction of the disappearing man before following Norman.

"Miss Katie, do you have any idea what a rare find this is?"

Katie nodded. "I think so."

"It's not everyday you see a cave dweller in a modern city."

"But how are we going to study him?"

"The same way we've studied everything else," Norman said. "We'll have a chat with your grandmother and see if we can't free up some time in the next while and we'll get to work. We'll document when he rises, where he goes, what he eats, when he sleeps, how he spends his spare time. We'll inspect his dwelling when he's not at home. And we'll catalogue all our data in a journal. Sound like fun?"

"Sounds like a lot of fun."

As they passed through the trail exit that opened up into Churchill Park, Norman pointed at a nearby sign for the Royal Botanical Gardens that stated Cootes Paradise was home to fifty species of birds and ground dwelling mammals.

"Think we should change the sign to read fifty-one?" Norman said, winking at Katie.

Katie giggled. "Maybe we should."

"And maybe I should gobble you up right now," said William, to himself, watching Katie from his black Volvo parked a few metres away in the parking lot outside the Aviary in Churchill Park.

To Be Continued . . .

William had seen Katie and her grandfather walking into the woods more than half an hour ago; had, in fact, been following Katie since spotting her talking to an old woman outside Second Cup, gasping with delight when he saw what she was wearing, then beaming with pride when he witnessed her preventing Natasha from being hit by a motorcycle (my darling little heroine), sneering at the ungrateful Natasha for yelling at Katie, glad they decided to part ways since this made it easier for him to follow Katie to her home on South Oval Street where he had watched Katie sitting on one of the benches on the front lawn of her house as she quietly observed the birds eating from a nearby feeder, until she suddenly sprang off the bench, smiling and waving and running down the street in response to seeing her grandfather, Norman, walking towards her with his dog Lucky. A few minutes later, after Norman had put Lucky in the house, William continued following Norman and Katie at a safe distance as they made their way up Newton Avenue, past the TCBY, to Churchill Park. Of course, when they entered the forest, William decided to wait for them in the parking lot outside the Aviary, preferring the air-conditioned sanctuary of his Volvo.

"Oh, my," William said, aloud, closing his eyes, suddenly queasy with arousal.

A delicious swirl of Katie's vanilla perfume — drafted by the slight afternoon breeze — had just wafted through the open sunroof of the Volvo, sending a sensuous shiver through his body.

William had a keen sense of smell, much keener than anyone he'd ever met. Except, of course, his twin brother. They attributed it to being raised in an uncommonly clean, almost antiseptic home, oftentimes amusing themselves for hours by opening their bedroom window a fraction of an inch and having competitions to see who could detect the most odours, as well as their origins.

It had taken William almost an entire Saturday afternoon of sampling vanilla-scented perfumes and essential oils at nearly a dozen different stores throughout the city before he found the exact one that Katie was wearing. After purchasing a bottle, William immediately returned to his apartment and washed his bed linen, sprinkling a few drops of the perfume in the water during the final rinse cycle and on a previously unscented dryer sheet before transferring the linens to the dryer. That night, after making his bed, he'd had several virile dreams, eventually waking up during his second nocturnal emission.

William sniffed the air several times, bathing his nostrils in the sweet vanilla scent. A fresh pang of pleasure pulsed through his genitals and he slowly slid his left hand into the pocket of his silk trousers.

Although he didn't own a dog (they were too messy), he had read that tied-up or housebound dogs were sometimes driven insane by their inability to investigate the origins of the smells reaching their olfactory senses. A particular smell — say, of a female dog in heat or some trespassing animal — would trigger deep-seated, primordial instincts in the dogs. Prevented from obeying or fulfilling these instincts because of being tied up or confined indoors, some dogs actually went crazy.

"We humans are the same way," William wrote in his diary, after reading the article. "What we're now doing to our pets, we've already done to ourselves. Instead of preventing the exploration of their natural tendencies or feeding them Prozac and Ritalin in an attempt to further domesticate them, we should return them — and us — to a state of nature. Instead of constantly having to rein in our instincts and natural tendencies, we should release them and allow them to govern us in an effort to be more pure, wholesome, and free."

Ever since he was an adolescent, William had been aware of his natural tendencies. Acutely aware of them. And, after his mother's death a few years ago, he ceased reining them in. "The corrupt psychiatric establishment may say I am sick, that I suffer from an illness, that I need to be cured. But what do they know? These are the same ignorant people who, as late as the 1970s, still considered homosexuality a disease."

William understood it was only a matter of time before people would understand that what he'd done, what he was doing and who he was, was perfectly natural. Perfectly normal.

"You're losing her, William," he said to himself, immediately starting the car and inching out of the parking lot, his left hand now vigorously massaging his genitals, his eyes riveted to the yellow sundress Katie was wearing.

He'd bought it for her while on a trip to Chicago two months ago, sending it to her in the mail, the accompanying note stating the dress was from her 'Secret Admirer.' Today was the first day he'd seen her wearing it, replacing her usual hiking boots, jeans, and T-shirt that he thought made her look far too boorish, boyish, and bourgeois.

"She looks so feminine, so girlish, so refined," he said aloud, now driving slowly along Dalewood Crescent, gazing longingly through the front windshield at Katie as she skipped along the sidewalk next to Norman, imagining himself slipping off her yellow sundress and slowly running his tongue over her soft, young flesh.

As he pulled the car alongside her, William eased his tongue out of his mouth and slowly licked the inside of the driver's-side tinted window, abruptly quickening the pace on his massage when he heard Katie giggle, her soft cheeks sprouting tiny dimples.

Accelerating past them, William continued watching Katie in the side- and rear-view mirrors as he crossed over Sterling Avenue, pulling his car across to the left-side curb, halfway between Sterling Avenue and King Street, intent on timing her arrival at his window with his impending orgasm.

Though William had watched Katie for nearly three months

now, he'd never done something like this before. In fact, everything about his relationship with Katie was different. His usual method of meeting women was much more straightforward and immediate. If he saw someone he liked, he would immediately pursue her. Katie, however, had required a more subtle approach. More planning. More surveillance.

Through the high-powered Bushnell telescope set up in his apartment, William had spent hours watching Katie dressing and undressing in her bedroom, eating breakfast in the kitchen, getting homeschooled in the sunroom, playing badminton and weeding the garden in the backyard with her grandmother, or walking to the corner store with Natasha.

He'd also spent a considerable amount of time in the past couple of months getting to know her and her grandparents in other ways, most notably by searching through their garbage late at night, which had furnished him with all sorts of valuable information, including a few of Katie's Favourite Things, which he had noted in his diary:

Food: Pad Thai

Beverage: Allen's apple juice

Snack: Strawberry Fruit-to-Go

Dessert: her grandmother's homemade date squares

Musician (female): Sarah McLachlan (also her mother's)

Musician (male): The Beatles (also her father's)

Clothing Store: Terra Ware Hemp store in Dundas

Toothpaste: 'Tom's of Maine'

TV Show: David Suzuki's *The Nature of Things*

Book: *Animal Farm*, by —

"Oh, here she comes," William said, aloud, simultaneously quickening the pace on his massage and sliding the driver's side window down two inches, knowing that a whiff of her scent as she passed by would be enough to guarantee his climax.

As she drifted past his window, William sniffed the air, quickly, rabidly, several times, before inhaling slowly, deeply, drinking in her intoxicatingly sweet —

William stopped massaging himself. He breathed in again, his nostrils filtering the air, his olfactory nerves quickly analyzing the various scents, focussing on one in particular.

"It can't be," he said. "Please, no. Not yet."

He closed his eyes, praying he'd made a mistake. After breathing in again, however, he quickly withdrew his left hand from his trousers.

"Oh, Katie. My dear, sweet, succulent, Katie. How could you?" he said, starting to weep.

The odour had been faint, almost undetectable, yet it was there — the undertones of blood swirling through her vanilla perfume and perspiration. Katie was menstruating.

In all his research, William had not, until this very moment, found any evidence to suggest Katie had begun to menstruate. In fact, all evidence indicated the contrary.

"Why the hell did you wait so long?" William said, glaring at himself in the rear-view mirror. "She was perfect. Untainted. Unadulterated. And now, now she's gone and turned herself into this, this — oh, what am I supposed to do now?" he said, slamming his hand down on the steering wheel.

The thought of starting over, of finding someone new, repulsed William. This was not how it was supposed to be. He was not supposed to spend all this time and energy on Katie, on getting to know her, on finding ways to be close to her, only to have her turn on him when he was only a few days away from making his final move. It wasn't fair. It wasn't right. Not after all he'd sacrificed. Not after he'd risked being caught sneaking into her backyard so he could sniff her clothes hanging outside on the clothesline. Not after he'd followed her nearly every day, watched out for her, made certain she always remained safe. And especially not after he'd reduced himself to rifling through her garbage every week for the past few months. No, this was not how it was supposed to be. Katie was not supposed to behave like this.

"You bitch," William growled through his tears, suddenly feeling a remorseless rage sluicing through his veins. "You stinky filthy little bitch! How could you do this to me?!"

Fixing his gaze on Katie, William put the car into drive and accelerated towards her, his eyes boring into her back. The front bumper of the Volvo was a mere ten metres from her when he heard the police siren.

To Be Continued . . .

GDP boost

"Pull over."

"What?"

"Pull over."

"Why?"

"Because there's a cop car with its lights flashing directly behind you."

"Oh, shit. Why didn't you tell me sooner?"

"I did but you were too busy talking you didn't hear me."

Geoff pulled the Jetta over to allow the police cruiser to pass and once the cruiser was in front of him said, "Seriously, Jennifer, you've *got* to listen to this."

"Geoff, news flash, the only thing I've got to listen to right now is John Coltrane," Jennifer replied, pushing PLAY on the car's CD player and turning up the volume.

"Please?" Geoff said, turning down the volume as they drove past Perry's, the restaurant where he and Jennifer had their first date.

"Can't this wait?" Jennifer said, sighing. "I need to unwind."

"Come on, hon, please. It's really quite stimulating."

"I don't want stimulating, Geoff. I want relaxing. I just worked another six-day week. I've got a ton of work to do tonight before I go to this seminar tomorrow and, to top it all off, you were twenty minutes late picking me up."

Her car, a candy apple red VW bug, had been in her uncle's shop since Wednesday. Geoff had been picking her up after work the last few days.

"I mean, you had the day off. Why were you late?"

"Well, there's a perfectly good reason for that, which is what I've been trying to tell you. I was in Coles bookstore in Jackson Square getting you that book you wanted and I met this really interesting guy. His name's Kyle and, well, I actually invited him over to our place for dinner tomorrow."

Jennifer gave him a puzzled look. "You do realize your parents are coming to dinner tomorrow, right?"

"Yeah, I remem —" Geoff said, stopping in mid-sentence in response to Jennifer's raised eyebrow and disbelieving expression. "Okay, I forgot. But it's no biggie. Kyle can come. It's not like it's an important dinner or anything. Besides, my parents will get a kick out of him."

"Whatever. They're *your* parents," Jennifer said, shaking her head. "So, is he homeless?"

Nearly every week Geoff regaled her with stories of some bum or bag lady or street kid with whom he'd had a chat or to whom he'd given a muffin or a cup of coffee. She figured it was only a matter of time before he invited one over for dinner.

"Not sure if he's homeless or not, actually. He was wearing this really expensive suit but you could tell it hadn't been dry-cleaned in a while, and his shirt was —"

"Geoff, I'm not that interested in what the guy was wearing."

"Just thought I'd give you a visual."

"Not required," Jennifer replied, now looking at Westdale High School. It was where she'd met Geoff. They were volunteering at the high school as ESL tutors during their third year at McMaster University. They'd been together ever since.

"Okay, well, can I at least tell you about him, then?"

"If you must."

"Great. So, anyway, the guy, Kyle, starts telling me a little bit about his life and how he was in Toronto and stopped to listen to this guy who —"

"Is this necessary?"

"It's background."

Jennifer raised her eyebrow again.

"Trust me. It's necessary," Geoff said, braking for the lights at Main and Macklin.

Jennifer sighed, then waved her hand, indicating he could continue, annoyed at herself for forgetting to renew her prescription, that Geoff's story would've been considerably more bearable after popping a Valium.

"Okay, so Kyle starts telling me about how he stopped to listen to some guy on a street corner in Toronto a few months ago and how the guy totally changed his life by telling him —"

"Oh my God. Geoff, please don't tell me this Kyle person got converted by some evangelical Christian standing outside the Eaton Centre yelling at people and handing out 'The End is Near' pamphlets."

"No. The guy was nothing like that. He was talking about our economy and started telling Kyle how the biggest problem with our economic system is that it relies on the GDP to determine our progress, believing that as long as our country's GDP is on the rise we'll have a prosperous economy. Now, according to this guy, the reason this is such a big problem is because most people don't realize what causes the GDP to rise. And that's where things get a little scary because the GDP actually rises each time there's something like a traffic accident or a couple gets divorced or someone goes to prison — and it rises a whole lot whenever there's a tsunami or a building gets bombed or a chunk of rainforest gets chopped down to make room for a huge vacation resort or a country goes to war. And the reason it rises is because these activities generate money. And so the more these things happen the better it is for the economy. Which is why these types of things are given a *high* value in our economy. And the crazy part about this is whenever people do stuff like ride a bike or take public transportation instead of using a car or decide to spend the weekend volunteering or with their family and neighbours instead of working or out at the casino gambling, it *slows* the GDP. And that's because these activities don't generate much money and so they're not really good for the economy and so they're given a *low* value. Only those things which involve an economic exchange are valued — which is why child care centres are valued but stay-at-home mothers aren't and why private schools are valued but home schooling isn't and why prisons-for-profit are valued but restorative justice programs aren't, why personal trainers and fitness clubs are valued but going for a hike or a run —"

"Geoff?"

"Yes?"

"I get the point."

"Oh. Okay. So, around this time Kyle started telling me that he was so excited to hear about this new way of measuring economic progress called the GPI, which stands for Genuine Progress Indicator, and which is something that takes into account way more things. Like according to this GPI thing, having an increase in car accidents or pollution or clear-cutting rainforests or gambling addictions or having people on medication to treat ulcers or stress or depression *isn't* a good thing — they're *not* things to be valued. Which is why the GPI sees these sorts of things as costs, *not* benefits. And it also looks at the Earth's resources for what they really are — *finite* — and then determines which uses are the most beneficial for these resources — not in terms of stimulating the exchange of money or improving the GDP but in terms of sustainability. Like, it totally goes against the GDP's idea of constant productivity and growth equals progress and —"

"Do we need anything at the grocery store?" Jennifer said, interrupting him as they approached the traffic lights at Dundurn and Main.

"We just went shopping yesterday," Geoff replied, looking into Fortinos Plaza.

"I know. I just thought we forgot a couple of things."

"You want to go?"

"No, forget it. It's alright. Go on with your story."

After proceeding through the lights at Dundurn, Geoff continued his story. "The really cool thing about the GPI is that leisure time has been totally worked into the assessment of a valuable life. Like say, for instance, that you're this big CEO guy making like two million dollars a year and you live in some huge house and drive a Porsche 911 Carrera but you don't have time to spend with your family or to read a book or visit your neighbours or get involved in the community, the GPI thing would say that you're not healthy, that you're not living a rich or valued life. Which is precisely what Aristotle said something like 2,400 years ago, about how leisure time was totally necessary. And he wasn't talking about the kind of leisure time where you can spend more time sitting around sucking on the TV or computer, or going on a dozen vacations or doing more shopping or playing golf fifteen times a week. He was talking about the kind of leisure that enabled you to become a whole person — things like reading and contemplating and discussing and debating things with your family and neighbours, being an active member in the community and really getting involved in the whole political process. And that's why we've got to get rid of the GDP as the indicator of progress or of a healthy economy or a healthy life and start using this GPI thing; we've got to stop valuing things that actually harm us and the planet and begin valuing those things that make us and the planet healthier. And, until we do that, we'll never have an accurate idea of what it means to have a healthy, successful life.'"

"Is that it?" Jennifer asked.

Geoff nodded.

"Can I listen to some music now?"

Geoff chuckled. "That's it? That's all you have to say? I mean, didn't any of this make sense to you?"

"Maybe. I mean, sure, of course it does, Geoff. It's just that who has time for this type of thing anymore?"

"What's that supposed to mean?"

"What it means is, when we were in university we had time to sit around debating these kinds of things but now we're — watch out!"

When Geoff saw what Jennifer was pointing at, he slammed on the brakes and swerved into the adjacent lane, narrowly avoiding the car making a right onto Locke Street.

"Sheesh," he said. "That was close."

"Hey, look on the bright side," Jennifer said, turning up the volume on the car's CD player. "You almost got in an accident and gave the GDP a boost."

"Very funny. You should —"

"Learn how to drive, moron!"

To Be Continued . . .

this is Toronto

"Shakil? Shakil? . . . Oh my God, what happened? . . . Did he signal? . . . What a jerk. All I heard was the sound of screeching tires and then you yelling, 'Learn how to drive, moron!' . . . Are you okay? You sure? . . . I'm going to let you go now . . . Because you're driving and the streets are obviously busy and I don't want you to get in an accident because you're talking to me on your cell phone. Just call me after you've talked to the owner, okay? . . . I love you . . . Bye."

Simone hung up the phone.

"What happened?" Hilary asked.

"Some jerk cut into his lane without signalling."

"Is he alright?"

"He's fine."

"Where is he?"

"In Hamilton."

"What's he doing in Hamilton?"

"I think he's playing in some bar in Hess Village tonight."

"You *think* he's playing?"

"Well, it's not for sure. Shakil's friend is supposed to be meeting him there. He knows the owner."

Hilary gave Simone a look, the look she gave whenever she thought Simone could do better than Shakil.

"It's a good opportunity," Simone said, frowning at Hilary. "It's always really busy there in the summer. It'll be great exposure."

"Providing he gets the gig."

"Well, yeah."

"And what are the chances of that?"

Simone shrugged. "His friend, the guy who knows the owner, said the owner owes him a favour, so, who knows? Fingers crossed."

"So it's not even close to a sure thing then, is it?"

"Well, it's pretty difficult to get a gig anywhere these days. There's a lot of competition."

"Hasn't that been my point all along? If it's that difficult to get a gig, maybe Shakil should just give it up and get a real job."

"He already has a real job."

"Simone. He's a waiter. Part time."

"Why do you have to be like this?"

"Like what?"

"So negative."

"I'm not negative. I'm pragmatic, which naturally comes across as negative to an idealist such as yourself."

"And what's wrong with having ideals?"

"Nothing, as long as they're realistic."

Simone shook her head. "Realistic ideals. Isn't that an oxymoron?"

"Not to a pragmatist. Besides, Shakil needs to start doing something with his life besides waiting tables."

"He's trying. Almost every day of the week he's out there, trying to line something up. At least he's not sitting on his ass or moping around the apartment all day, talking about what a great musician he could've been."

"Simone, honey. I'm not questioning Shakil's motivation or his drive. It's just that he's not getting any younger."

"What's that supposed to mean?"

"It means that he's thirty-six and that if he was going to make it as a musician, he should've made it by now."

"It's not something that happens overnight, you know."

"Oh come on, Simone. He's been playing guitar and singing his songs for almost twenty years now and he's no further ahead now than he was when he started. He's entered every Battle of the Bands, every singing and songwriting contest humanly possible and never won anything. All I'm saying is it might be time for him to re-evaluate things."

"But he absolutely *loves* his music."

"I know he does. And everything else in his life takes a back seat to music, including you."

"That's not true."

"Right. So then why is he in Hamilton trying to convince some club owner to let him play a few songs instead of spending the day with you? Not only is it your *birthday*, but it also just happens to be your only day off during the entire week."

"But this is important to him. He needs this."

"I know he does. All I'm saying is that you're thirty-three and if you want to buy a house, get married, and have kids like you're always telling me you do, it's probably not going to happen with Shakil."

"What, now you're my psychic?"

"Simone, I'm not saying Shakil's a bad guy. In fact, I happen to think he's a great guy. But face it, he doesn't want the same things as you do."

"That's not true."

"Simone, it is. You went from being his groupie to being his girlfriend to being his patron. You're the best thing that's ever happened to Shakil and he still treats you like, well, like you're still a groupie."

Simone sighed.

"You deserve better."

"Oh, I don't know. Maybe you're right, maybe I should —"

"Look at this town," Hilary said, grabbing hold of Simone's arm and gesturing to the pubs and patios and pedestrians along King Street West. "This is Toronto. There are tens of thousands of great men out there just dying to meet someone like you."

"Whatever."

"I'm serious."

"Like who?"

"Like my friend Sheldon. He absolutely adores you."

"Hilary, you told me last year that Sheldon is the biggest player you know."

"Was. He told me last month he's ready to settle down now. He's tired of the game and wants to trade his condo, Beamer, and golf clubs in for a house, a Volvo, and a baby stroller."

"I wish him the best."

"Well, how about Robert? He's available."

"Robert Herron? He's married."

Hilary shook her head. "Divorced. Three weeks ago. Got to keep the house *and* the yacht."

"I've never really seen myself with someone who was divorced."

"Well, then. How about Sanjay?"

"Sanjay Choudhury?"

"Uh-huh. He's been asking about you for months."

"Really?"

"Yes. And when I told him it was your birthday today and that I was taking you out he practically begged me to tell him where we were going tonight so he could meet us there."

"Are you serious?"

"Completely."

"What did you tell him?"

"I told him to take a number."

"You didn't."

"I did."

"Why haven't you mentioned this before?"

"Because I was waiting for you to be ready to break up with —"

"Oh, hang on," Simone said, interrupting Hilary. "It's my cell phone. It's probably Shakil calling me back. I'll just be a minute."

"What do you want me to do about Sanjay?"

"I don't know," Simone said, shrugging. "Did he really say he wanted to meet us somewhere tonight?"

Hilary nodded.

"Well, maybe you should give him a call then."

Hilary smiled. "Will do."

Simone hit the TALK button on her cell phone. "Hi, honey. How'd it go?"

To Be Continued . . .

the surprised look

"Um, actually, the owner isn't here yet . . . I don't know. Apparently he left a message saying he'd be back in a couple of hours . . . Um, yeah, probably . . . I might as well. I mean, I'm here now. It'd be great to play here tonight. It's already packed . . . I don't know, I hope he does. I'll probably give him until 9:00, maybe 10:00 p.m. or so and then I'll . . . what? . . . It is? . . . Okay, well, call me back after you recharge it, okay? . . . Okay."

Shakil pushed the END button on his cell phone, ordered a Corona from the waitress and plopped down on one of the patio chairs at 33 Hess. Leaning back in his chair, he began absorbing the carnival ambience of Hess Village, surveying the large, animated throngs of people shuffling along the bricked streets, streaming into the various bars — Elixir, Gown & Gavel, Polos, Ivorys, The Sidebar — joining the already standing or already seated, who were merrily sipping drinks, laughing, posing, and/or grooving to the swanky music spewing into the late afternoon air.

After spending a few moments visually tailing a young woman, the kind of young woman that used to come out to watch him play years ago, Shakil abruptly got up and walked into the washroom. Fortunately, the only stall was unoccupied and he went inside, closed the door, secured the latch, closed his eyes, and started to cry.

He had heard about this sort of thing happening to other musicians, he just thought that it wouldn't happen to him, that he wouldn't have to one day face the realization that he was never going to make it, that his dream of being discovered by some talent scout or signed to a major record label would forever be just that — a dream.

For the next few minutes he compiled a mental inventory of his life as a musician, the years of practise he'd put in, the numerous bands he'd started and abandoned; how, in his mid-twenties, already tired of arguing and relying on increasingly unreliable band mates, he'd decided to go it alone; how this decision, initially, had proven to be the right one, as he ended up getting a few more gigs and a lot more attention, especially from women; and how, as his mid-twenties turned into his early-thirties, fewer and fewer women thought he was cool — just as fewer and fewer club owners wanted him to play in their clubs.

After nearly five minutes of uninterrupted crying, Shakil finally opened his eyes and the first thing he saw was a blurry, pale green folded sheet of paper on the tiled floor next to the toilet. Normally, given his surroundings, Shakil wouldn't have even considered picking it up but, seeing as he wasn't feeling all that normal at the moment, he bent over and scooped the paper off the floor.

After wiping his eyes on his sleeve a couple of times, he unfolded the piece of paper, immediately saw that it was a wedding speech, and started reading it, quickly, skimming over the first few paragraphs until he reached the part where the man was thanking his wife:

". . . I used to think I knew what it meant to feel, but that meaning is a mere shadow of what I now feel as a result of having been with you. You have brought so much fulfilment, so much happiness, into my life, it's indescribable. You know what I feel like? I feel like the Grinch when he's on top of that mountain above the town of Whoville and he's about to chuck all the presents off the cliff and then something miraculous happens — his heart suddenly grows three times its normal size. That's how I feel since we've been together. Whenever I look at you I see everything — lover, best friend, mother of our child, and now, wife. You are my symphony, my poem, my muse, the woman I call 'home.' The only words that do you justice are these: to see yourself through my eyes, is to know what perfection looks like. I —"

"Excuse me."

Startled, Shakil stopped reading, noticing a pair of black dress shoes were now standing outside the door to the stall. A moment later, he heard a guy clear his throat, followed by a knock on the stall door and the same voice saying, "Excuse me."

"Yes?" Shakil said, once again wiping his eyes.

"Uh, this may seem like an odd question, but is there a green sheet of paper in there anywhere? It's probably folded up."

"Um, yeah."

"Oh, man. Thank God," the guy said. "You wouldn't mind passing it under the door, would you? It's my buddy's speech. He got married across the street, at The Wedding Chapel. We took him here for a couple of beers before saying 'I do' and now he's about an hour away from saying his speech and he's in a major panic. This was the last place he said to check."

"Well, here it is," Shakil said, quickly folding up the paper before holding it under the side of the stall.

"Thanks a lot," the guy said, taking the paper from Shakil. "My buddy owes you one."

As soon as Shakil heard the bathroom door close, he took his cell phone out of his pocket and began dialling Hilary's number, intent on finding out where Simone was going to be tonight, already imagining the surprised look on Simone's face when he walked into whatever bar she was in and —

"Hey, Hilary, how are you?"

To Be Continued . . .

food, dancing, men — whatever . . . .

"Fine, and you? . . . That's good. Can you hang on a sec? . . . Thanks."

Hilary covered her phone and whispered to Simone, "I've got to take this outside," before walking quickly out of Lush on Queen West, stealing a glance back at Simone to make certain she wasn't following her.

"What's up, Shakil?" Hilary said, now between two T-shirt vendors on Queen West. "Um, no, actually. She just said something came up and she had to go . . . No. No idea where she was headed . . . Sure, of course, I will. I think we're supposed to get together later on anyway so I'll call you as soon as I know anything, okay? . . . Okay. See you, Shakil."

"Who was that?" Simone asked when Hilary walked back into Lush.

"My ex," Hilary said.

"Really?"

"Yeah, he's still holding out hope."

"After six months?"

Hilary nodded. "Can you blame him?" she said, batting her eyes and striking a sexy pose.

Simone smiled. "Not at all. What did you tell him?"

"What I always do. Call me in a few days. I may have a change of heart."

"You did not."

"I did so."

"Oh my God. Hilary, you're horrible. No wonder he keeps hanging on."

"Hey, a girl needs to keep her options open," Hilary replied, and then, after inhaling the watermelon scent of a bar of soap, she asked, "Are we done here?"

Simone nodded. "I think so."

Taking hold of Simone's arm, Hilary led her out of the store. "So, girlfriend, where do you want to go tonight?"

"I hadn't really thought about it."

"Feel like having dinner?"

"Sure."

"Drinks?"

"Sure."

"Dancing."

"Um, yeah, okay."

"So what are you in the mood for?"

"You mean food-wise?"

"Food, dancing, men — whatever."

"Men?"

"Um, correct me if I'm wrong, Simone darling, but I believe we were standing at the corner of Peter and King when a certain someone suggested I give Sanjay Choudhury a call and tell him where we'd be tonight?"

Simone blushed. "Well, yeah, I know. But I've been thinking maybe it's better if we keep things kind of low-key."

"Screw low-key. I've got a better idea. For the next hour we're going to invite every cute guy we see to your birthday party."

Simone laughed. "It's a party now, is it?"

"Hey, you two," Hilary shouted at two guys seated on The Black Bull patio, "both of you are invited to this gal's birthday party tonight!"

. . . . To Be Continued . . .

I might . . . .

"Where's the party at?" Jeremy asked, grinning at the two women.

"Dinner at Saint Tropez at 7:00 p.m.!" the woman wearing the short skirt shouted back. "Followed by drinks at Rain!"

"I love both those places! We'll see you at 7:00 p.m.!" Jeremy replied. Then, raising his glass, he added, "Happy birthday, sweetie."

"Have you ever heard of Saint Tropez or Rain?" Derek asked Jeremy a few moments later.

"No. But I'm sure you have."

"Don't tell me you're actually thinking of going," Derek said to Jeremy.

Jeremy shrugged. "I might."

Derek shook his head in disbelief, wondering how Jeremy could be like this, especially since he was just saying —

"Now *that's* a nice ass."

To Be Continued . . .

well, *bye*

For a moment, Kristan thought about letting the 'Nice ass' comment slide. In fact, on any other day, she probably would've smiled to herself and added the comment to her inventory of daily compliments. She may even have glanced back and said, 'Thanks.' But today was different. Perhaps it was the warm weather or the fact that she'd got off the streetcar at the wrong stop and had been walking for almost five blocks now in her not-yet-broken-in strapped heels. Perhaps it was that while stepping off the streetcar she'd stepped in someone's still-steaming vomit. Perhaps it was that she hadn't even left Toronto yet and she was already twenty minutes late in meeting her sister, Stephanie, in Hamilton, who said she needed to speak with her — *right away.* Perhaps it was that she had just discovered — roughly eight hours ago in her recently renovated bathroom — that she was pregnant, a fact that would've made most married thirty-six-year-old women who wanted a child happy but, seeing as her only sexual partner in the past three months had been her sister Stephanie's fiancé, Jacobus, she wasn't all that thrilled about the news. Whatever the reason, today was different, and, even if she did have a nice ass, which she did, she wasn't in the mood to have it publicly acknowledged by a couple of slimy guys sitting on a patio and so, halting in mid-stride, she spun around on her heels and, using a suitably indignant tone of voice, said, "What did you just say?" noticing, as the words were leaving her mouth, that the two men seated on the patio outside The Black Bull were very cute, very well dressed, and not even remotely slimy.

"Excuse me?" one of them, the one wearing the mirrored glasses, said, smirking and pulling down his sunglasses, meeting Kristan's glare without blinking.

It was the self-satisfied smirk that made Kristan decide to continue glaring at him for a full five seconds — a technique she often employed in her job as an attorney to coerce confessions out of reluctant defenders — before turning her glare on the other one, immediately concluding that the man's eyes were so aquamarine blue he had to be wearing coloured contacts. When he looked away after only a split second, pretending to be interested in something across the street, Kristan placed her right hand on her hip, rolled her eyes and said, "Well, you two obviously didn't graduate from the same acting school."

The guy with the aquamarine blue eyes shifted uncomfortably in his seat before looking down and nudging a phantom pebble along the concrete with his leather, open-toed sandals.

"I'm sorry," the mirrored sunglasses guy said, still looking at Kristan above his sunglasses. "But do we *know* you?"

"Listen guys, cut the charade. I'm not going anywhere until I find out which one of you was the author of the oh-so-cerebral 'nice ass' comment."

Looking more than slightly bemused, the mirrored sunglasses guy snickered before he said, "I think maybe you're making a —"

"What, a mistake?" Kristan said, interrupting him. "Please. Don't even *try* to tell me it's *my* mistake now that *you're* being confronted," she added, her confidence bolstered by the growing interest from the other patrons on the patio.

"Okay, I confess," the mirrored sunglasses guy said, throwing up his hands, "I said it. But before you start telling me how rude or sexist or inappropriate my comment was, what makes you think I was referring to *your* ass?"

At that moment, Kristan noticed his right hand had casually drifted over to the aquamarine-blue-eyed man's left leg and was now caressing and squeezing it gently.

"Oh . . . I'm . . . I didn't," Kristan said, fumbling for something suitable to say, her gaze riveted to the mirrored sunglasses guy's hand. She felt her throat tightening. "I had no idea you were. I mean. I'm very, very —"

"Not a problem," said the mirrored sunglasses guy, "happens all the time."

"Really? Well . . . I'm still . . . you know."

"We know. By the way, love your shoes. Manolo Blahnik's?"

"Oh, um . . . thanks. And yes. They are. Again, I'm sorry. Really. I thought you were . . . Well, *bye.*"

"After meeting you, I wish I was," the mirrored sunglasses guy said, watching her facial expression indicate she was temporarily confused as to what he'd meant, before she broke out into a smile, nodding her head and gesturing as though she'd just got it before turning around and half-walking, half-running down the sidewalk in the direction of Starbucks.

. . . . To Be Continued . . .

I don't need luck

"You can take your hand off my leg now, Jeremy," Derek said, motioning towards his stepbrother's right hand. "She's gone."

Jeremy started laughing. "Now that," he said, removing his right hand from Derek's leg and slapping it down on the patio table, "was fucking priceless. I don't think I've ever heard so many attempted sentences in my entire life."

Derek half-smiled.

"Did you *see* the look on her face when I put my hand on your leg?" Jeremy said, giving Derek a nudge. "It was like two seconds before that moment she thought she had us and then, as soon as she saw my hand on your leg, wham! Her whole case collapsed."

"You sure fooled her," Derek said, half-heartedly.

Jeremy laughed. "Fuckin' eh, I did," he replied. Then, almost as an afterthought, he added, "You've got to admit, though. She did have a nice ass."

"I didn't notice."

"Really? What's wrong with your eyes, bro?"

Derek shrugged.

"She definitely works out. A woman doesn't have an ass like that at her age without spending some quality time in the gym. You ever see her when you're working out?" Jeremy asked while surveying, for probably the fifth time since meeting Derek at The Black Bull half an hour ago, his stepbrother's perfectly sculpted 6'2", 190-pound body, picturing him strutting his stuff down the runways in Toronto and New York — which he'd already done twice this year.

Derek shook his head. "How the hell did you know her shoes were Manolo Blahnik's?"

"Lucinda has the same pair."

The mentioning of Lucinda's name made the bottom fall out of Derek's stomach and a collage of images surge into his visual cortex — images of Lucinda trying on shoes, the sight of her ankles, her silken legs, the adorable tattoo of the Road Runner just above her left ankle.

"Speaking of Lucinda," Jeremy started to say, pausing in mid-sentence to watch a young woman in her late twenties walking on the opposite sidewalk, his gaze following her until she made her way inside The Gap. "Before we were distracted by the birthday babes and Ms. Nice Ass, where were we in 'The Attempted Seduction of Lucinda Lancaster'?"

"I had just picked her up."

"Right. So, you picked her up and the two of you drove here, right?"

Derek nodded his head.

"And then what?"

"And then I took her to all the places you said she'd like — Courage My Love, Millo, Banana Republic, Holt Renfrew, Chanel."

"Did she get anything?"

Derek nodded. "A pair of shoes at Millo. A purse and bracelet at Courage My Love and a skirt at Banana Republic."

"And you paid for it, right?"

Derek shook his head. "She wouldn't let me."

"What happened when you insisted?"

"She refused to buy them unless she paid."

"Seriously?"

Derek nodded.

Jeremy smiled. "Excellent," he said, pulling down his sunglasses a fraction to survey an oncoming group of women.

While Jeremy continued trawling the many women walking by the patio, Derek quickly reviewed the day he and Lucinda had spent together, how, after eating dinner at Marcel's he attempted to take her to see a concert at the Glenn Gould studio but she refused, saying she had promised to first visit the studio with Jeremy, so they instead saw a movie at the Paramount, browsing books and magazines at Chapters until the movie started, then strolling over to Rain afterwards for a couple of drinks followed by an hour of non-stop dancing at Indian Motorcycle Club before jumping back in the car and driving to the Beaches for a stroll along the boardwalk where the two of them spent another hour or so regaling each other with their childhood memories of skinny dipping and getting drunk on the beach as the fresh, lake air and her perfume — Attraction, by Lancôme — swirled around them, soaking deeper and deeper into Derek's memory.

As usual, the city had co-operated completely, making Derek feel, yet again, as though he was on the set of some giant movie production where everything magically came together. Derek loved Toronto. Loved it the same way he was sure some people loved sliding a fresh slice of mango into their mouth or having a cottage up north or slipping into a new pair of shoes. He loved how Toronto provided an almost inexhaustible list of possibilities, how a person's every desire could be fulfilled within the city's limits. It was the reason he'd moved to Toronto a few years ago and why he'd taken each of his stepbrother's girlfriends here to seduce them.

"And you're telling me nothing happened?" Jeremy was now asking, eyeing up an Asian girl wearing a beige jogging suit and '70s-style sunglasses walking with an Eminem look-a-like.

"Like I told you on the phone. I threw everything I had at her. Nothing worked."

Jeremy smiled. "You tried to get her back to your place?"

Derek nodded. "She wouldn't go for it."

"And you even invited her out again?"

"Four times over the next three days," he lied, "just like you wanted."

"And each time she refused?"

Derek nodded.

"You think if the two of you went out again she might fold?"

Derek shook his head.

"How can you be sure?"

"I just am."

It was something in his stepbrother's tone of voice that made Jeremy look away from the Asian girl and glance at Derek. Since the age of sixteen, after having an affair with his father's third fiancée — a twenty-six-year-old trophy his father had picked up while vacationing in the Dominican Republic with Derek's mother — Derek hadn't had sex with a woman who wasn't attached. The two of them had been planning the seduction of Jeremy's girlfriend, Lucinda, for almost a month, ever since Jeremy found himself entertaining the idea of proposing to her. It was the fourth time Jeremy had used his stepbrother in this capacity, the previous three times resulting in Jeremy breaking up with his girlfriend the following day.

He was certain Derek didn't mind. In fact, Derek sometimes referred to himself as 'Man's instrument.' In the same way that a minister referred to himself as God's instrument, to be used in a manner that God saw fit, Derek considered himself to be 'Man's instrument,' to be used in matters of fidelity in order to weed out the weak. He was a test that women needed to pass. And so far, no woman had. Until Lucinda.

Jeremy had planned everything down to the last detail. He'd made certain Lucinda wasn't menstruating, that she knew he was going to be in Montreal for no less than five days, possibly even a week; he'd arranged for Derek, on her day off, to take her shopping, then to a great restaurant, then to the Glenn Gould studio or, if she refused, to her favourite type of movie, then out dancing — all things he wasn't particularly fond of.

"Something wrong, bro?" Jeremy said, now looking at his stepbrother with a mixture of relief and pity, having concluded that the reason Derek was bummed out was because Lucinda had rejected him.

Derek shook his head. "Je suis un peu fatigué, mais ça va," he said, half-lying. Though he was a little tired, he was far from alright. The truth was, he'd fallen for Lucinda. The moment she refused to have him pay for her dinner, he noticed the change in himself. No longer did he elicit the contrived laughter or smiles or enthusiasm he normally would as part of his performance. His act disappeared and he started enjoying her, enjoying them, enjoying how he felt around her — so much so that by the time they'd reached the boardwalk he was wondering how she could end up with someone who hires a person to try and sleep with his would-be fiancée.

"Relax, bro. You can't win 'em all," Jeremy said, giving him a pat on the back. "So, how much do I owe you?"

"Nothing. Lucinda paid me for everything already."

"Really?"

Derek nodded. "She paid me for dinner and drinks and the movie right away. When we got to Oakville she asked me to stop off at an ATM and gave me another forty bucks when I dropped her off, saying it was for the last couple of drinks, gas, and anything else she might have missed."

"Wow."

Derek nodded, then considered telling his stepbrother that Lucinda had then said, "You know, Derek, I don't think I've had a better time in all my life," but before he could tell her that he'd felt the same way, she'd added, "Please don't ever call me again," her words ripping right through him.

"So," Derek said, scratching the back of his head, suddenly itching to be rid of his stepbrother. "When did you tell Lucinda you'd be back in Oakville?"

Jeremy checked his watch. "In a few hours," he replied. Then, noticing his stepbrother cringing, he asked, "You sure you're okay, bud?"

Derek considered saying it, telling Jeremy that he was in love with Lucinda. But he couldn't. Jeremy would probably laugh, tell him he was just feeling this way because she wouldn't have sex with him, that he was suffering from 'finally-being-rejected-equals-true-love' syndrome or something of the sort.

"I'm fine," Derek replied. "By the way, when are you planning to propose to her?"

"Probably tonight."

"Really?"

Jeremy nodded. "I've got the ring in the car."

"The same one?"

"Yep. Fourth time's the charm, I guess."

Derek smiled, weakly.

"Well, bro, I suppose I should probably get going," Jeremy said, rising up from his seat and extending his hand towards Derek, "What can I say? Thanks again."

"No problem," Derek replied, shaking his stepbrother's hand. "Good luck tonight."

"Hey, I don't need luck. I've got you," he said, slapping Derek on the back before walking towards the exit of The Black Bull.

Derek watched Jeremy stride like a peacock over to his car, get in, honk twice, wave, and pull away from the curb outside The Black Bull. Derek shook his head at his stepbrother's luck. The entire street was jammed, not a parking spot for blocks — yet five seconds before Jeremy arrives, someone pulls out of a free parking spot only fifteen feet from where they were meeting.

Derek sighed, dropping his head into his hands, his still-open eyes catching sight of two ants play-fighting on the cement beneath his feet, playfully nudging and bumping into one another, circling around and around as though they were dance partners or potential combatants, immediately reminding him of his mother and her husband, Vincent.

Still watching the ants, he withdrew the cell phone from his front pocket and started dialling their number.

To Be Continued . . .

it's no joke . . . .

"Vincent, where's the phone?" Sonia shouted, startling her husband, who was just entering the house, his arms cradling two bags of groceries.

"How in blazes should I know?" Vincent replied, kicking off his deck shoes, "I've been at the market all afternoon."

"Well, don't just stand there like a sack of groceries, help me find it. We've only got two more rings before the answering machine picks up!"

"Oh, my God," Vincent said, now staring at Sonia, horror-stricken. "What the hell have you done to your hair?"

"Thanks for noticing," Sonia said, now searching under a pile of clothes in the living room for the phone.

"I'd have to be legally blind not to notice," Vincent replied, setting down the groceries on the kitchen island.

"Darn," Sonia said, snapping her fingers, "too late," referring to the phone. Then, turning back to Vincent, she primped her hair and asked, "So, what do you think?"

Vincent shook his head in disbelief. "What's it called, the 'raped and pillaged' look?"

"Ah," Sonia said, raising her eyebrows and smiling, "I take it you like it, then?"

"What's wrong with the way you had it last week?"

"I got tired of it."

"In one week?"

"What can I say, I'm fond of change."

"Do you even remember what your *real* hair colour is?"

"Real is so passé, darling. Now, where is that darn phone?"

"Why don't you just hit the locator button on the base?"

"It takes all the adventure out of trying to find it."

"Sonia, I don't understand why you can't —"

"How was the market?"

"Exquisite."

Sonia chuckled at both her successful redirection of Vincent and his response. "What is it with you and that place?"

Vincent shrugged. "One man's market is another woman's hair salon."

"Touché," Sonia said, smiling as she recalled how she'd met Vincent at the St. Lawrence Market. He was giving a cooking demonstration, something to do with fish. Or maybe it was chicken? Pork? She could never remember. At any rate, nearly everyone in the crowd gathered around his portable kitchen seemed to know him or had heard of him. She hadn't the faintest idea who he was.

"What's all the fuss about?" she'd asked.

"Oh, isn't it exciting?" the woman standing beside her exclaimed. "I can't believe it's really him."

"Who?"

"Vincent the Vagabond."

"That's his name?"

"Oh, heavens, no," the woman standing on the other side of her had replied, smiling and shaking her head. "Vincent VoorAllen is his name. *Vincent the Vagabond* was the name of his restaurant."

In the next few minutes Sonia would learn that Vincent VoorAllen was a third-generation chef who, after leaving his native Holland at seventeen, had spent the next fifteen years travelling through Europe, the Middle East, and even parts of Africa and the Far East, working as a sous-chef and developing a keen appreciation of each country's spices, sauces, chutneys, and cooking styles before immigrating to the United States and opening a restaurant in Pennsylvania called *Vincent the Vagabond*.

"His restaurant was in all the tourist guides in the '80s and '90s," a man behind her said, popping his head over her shoulder. "My wife and I ate there twice. We even have a signed menu."

"He's practically a legend in the culinary industry," the woman in front of her said, adding, after a sigh of exhilaration, "Did you know that he was partially responsible for introducing nouvelle cuisine in the '80s and starting the fusion craze in the late '90s?"

"Really," Sonia replied, not the least bit impressed. "So what's he doing in Toronto?"

"Community service," Vincent had replied, smiling at Sonia from his perch behind the mobile kitchen, having overheard their entire conversation. "I was caught stealing a baguette and some smoked salami in the market here and one of your city judges sentenced me to three cooking shows a day for the next two weeks."

What he was really doing in Toronto, she discovered a few hours after accepting his invitation to dinner, was visiting family. His older brother had immigrated to Canada, settling in Toronto after a three-month stay in Ottawa.

"I thought you said you were going to vacuum the rug today," Vincent was now saying, pointing at the large Persian area rug in the living room still coated with hairs from Sonia's cat, Theodore.

"I got rid of it," Sonia replied, still searching for the phone.

"The cat?"

"No, silly," Sonia said, shaking her head. "The vacuum."

"The vacuum?"

Sonia nodded. "Yesterday. Didn't I tell you?"

Stunned, Vincent remained on mute for a few moments before saying, "No. I guess it must have slipped your mind."

"Well, in case *this* slips my mind, I'd better tell you right now I'm getting rid of the rug, too."

"I beg your pardon?"

"In fact, I'm getting rid of all our rugs tomorrow. And I'm having the carpets removed next week."

"What are you talking about?"

"Remember that famous quote by what's-his-name, the guy who said, 'Nature abhors a vacuum'?"

"I believe it was Albert Einstein."

"Well, whoever it was, yesterday I realized that no one abhors a vacuum more than I do. So I got rid of it. And when I got rid of it, I suddenly realized there was no sense in keeping our rugs and carpeting if we have nothing to clean them."

Vincent shook his head. "Unbelievable."

Sonia smiled. "Besides, our home will be a lot healthier now. Do you have any idea how many harmful chemicals are in carpets?"

"I'm afraid to ask."

"Well, then, you shouldn't have bought me the book."

"What book?"

"The book that says one of the healthiest things you can do for your home is to get rid of your carpets."

"Sonia, I did not buy you a book that instructed you to get rid of our carpets."

"Well, indirectly you did. You bought me a gift certificate from Chapters which I used to buy the book, *Living Healthy in a Toxic World*."

"Please God," Vincent said, clapping his hands together and looking up, "help me."

"Vincent, my name is Sonia, and I'm not up there, I'm right over here. Besides, as you've reminded me every time I mention God's name, Nietzsche declared Him to be dead a long time ago."

"You do realize you're absolutely mad, don't you?"

Sonia smiled. "I've had my suspicions."

"Just once I'd like to come home without discovering you've rearranged something in our house or on your body."

"If that happened you'd probably leave me the very next day. Besides, I thought you loved my spontaneity."

"Spontaneity is one thing. But this borders on multiple personality disorder."

"I believe the official term is now Dissociative Identity Disorder."

"Well, whatever it is, you're certainly a candidate."

"I can't see that being a bad thing."

"And why not?"

"I've heard most men enjoy variety in their women. With me you've got it all in one woman. The thirty-three faces of Sonia."

"Well, I'm not most men. I prefer my women with only one face."

"Ah, finally, here it is," Sonia said, triumphantly holding up the portable phone. "Between the cushions in the beige sofa. Right where you left it."

"Sonia, neither of us have sat in that sofa since Chrétien was in office."

"Precisely why you chose to hide it there, I'm sure," she said, giving Vincent a quick peck on the cheek. "One of your futile attempts to prevent me from 'ringing up an enormous long distance bill' in your absence, I suppose."

"Sonia, I did not —"

"Oh look, it was Derek who called. I'll have to see what he wants."

"Tell him to come over for dinner."

"I'll ask him. Though, he probably won't show up if he thinks you're cooking."

"Very funny, Sonia."

"It's no joke, Vincent. He still hasn't recovered from the last time you — oh, hi Derek. Sorry I missed you a while ago. I was looking for the phone. Vincent hid it on me . . . I'm completely serious. He's tired of me calling the psychic hotline . . . Of course, I do. I have to know whether he's going to abandon me for one of his cooking demonstration groupies. I swear if I died there'd be dozens of women at my funeral weeping tears of joy. So, how are you, Derek? Is everything all right? . . . What's the matter, dear? Are you having women troubles again? Is —"

. . . . **To Be Continued . . .**

this is crazy . . . .

"Mom. Mom! I think you're supposed to actually give me a chance to answer one of your questions before asking another . . . Yes, I'm fairly certain that's how it works. So, to answer your first and third questions — which are the only two I'm going to answer — I'm doing well and there's nothing the matter, I just didn't get enough sleep last night . . . Yes, that's the truth . . . No, there's nothing else going on. I called because I was simply wondering what you two were up to . . . That's the truth . . . So, what are you up to? . . . Really? . . . Um, yeah, sure. As long as Vincent's doing the cooking . . . I'm serious . . . Mom, the last time you tried to cook me something I thought I was going to have to get my stomach pumped. I'm not joking . . . Mom, you know you're a horrible cook . . . I'm *not* exaggerating. You should be thankful you found Vincent. He probably saved you thousands of dollars in TV dinners and medical bills . . . He is? Well, in that case, I'm in . . . What? No, I haven't seen him. Last I heard he was out of town . . . Montreal, I think . . . If I do, I'll tell him . . . Yes, I promise. You need me to pick something up? . . . You sure? . . . Okay. Then I'll see you in thirty minutes or so, depending on traffic."

Derek hung up the phone and continued to remain seated, unable to summon the requisite energy or motion to get up, his brain repeatedly relaying the message to his legs to stand up, his legs repeatedly ignoring the message, refusing to budge.

"If you ask me, I think he's hot."

Derek had smelled the perfume — Attraction, by Lancôme —

before hearing the words; had, in fact, immediately stood up and nearly lunged in the direction of the scent, his sudden movement startling a woman walking on the other side of the railing, her hands instinctively coming up in front of her face as though she were protecting herself from being hit.

"Oh shit. I'm sorry," Derek said, quickly pulling his hands away from the railing and holding them up while taking a step back, embarrassed by the 'What-the-hell-is-wrong-with-you?' expression on the woman's face. "I'm sorry," he said again. "I thought you were someone else."

Derek sat down and shook his head.

"This is crazy," he said, out loud. Then, after a few more moments of deliberation, he snatched up his cell phone from the patio table and began dialling a number.

. . . . **To Be Continued . . .**

well, well, well . . . .

"Hello? Hello? I can barely hear you," Lucinda said into her cell phone, pushing her way through an amoeba-like glob of people moving along Hess Village in Hamilton. "Hello? Hello? Are you there?"

Lucinda waited a few more moments, straining to hear something other than the static coming through her cell phone before saying, "If you're still there and you can hear this, I'm in Hamilton right now but I'll be back in Oakville in a couple of hours, probably by no later than 7:00 p.m. so you can try and reach me then. Okay? I'm hanging up now."

A moment after she'd hit the END button on her cell phone — thinking briefly that it had sounded like Derek, her boyfriend's stepbrother, on the other end of the phone — Lucinda quickened her pace to catch up to Rawnie and Lance.

"So, why do you feel sorry for Jason?" she asked Rawnie when she finally caught up to her and Lance just before they rounded the corner and began heading up George Street.

"I just think his career change is stupid."

"I don't think it's that bad," Lucinda replied. "Besides, this way he's actually making money. If he stuck with either of the other three he'd be going into debt by like a hundred thousand dollars."

"Well, first off, I'm not buying the whole 'going-into-debt-a-hundred-thousand-dollars-thing' because I'm fairly certain Jason's parents were paying for his education. And, secondly, if he actually remained with one of the other three jobs, he would've at least had the opportunity to help people."

"And pharmaceutical reps don't help people?"

"Well, yeah, they help giant pharmaceutical companies peddle drugs to consumers."

"Come on. They do more than that."

"Come on, yourself, Lucinda. A pharmaceutical rep is nothing more than a legalized drug pusher. I mean, Jason's job is to go around to doctors' offices and convince them to write prescriptions for his pharmaceutical company's drug. He does this by bribing them with things like free lunches, free dinners, an afternoon at a spa, front-row seats at sporting events, free weekend getaways for the doctor's family at some spa retreat, and, if the bribes work, the doctors end up writing scripts for his particular drug and if he gets enough doctors to do this, he gets a monetary bonus and/or a trip to the Caribbean at the end of the year."

"I take it you're not fond of his current choice of employment," Lucinda said.

"Who would be if they really knew what was going on? I mean, over a hundred thousand people in North America die each year because of complications with medications. And nobody really raises a stink. Of course, when there's one incident of someone thinking they've had a stroke because of a chiropractic adjustment the whole medical establishment is up in arms, crying foul. It's absolutely —"

"Well, well, well. If it isn't Rawnie DeVrais, CEO of the real EPA."

. . . . To Be Continued . . .

an AA meeting . . . .

Despite the fact that Rawnie was now regarding him as though he were an infectious disease, Adam smiled and said, "Just when I thought I'd had my fill of retro-inspired fashion, good ol' Rawnie DeVrais comes along."

"This isn't retro," Rawnie replied.

"What then, a fresh interpretation of grunge?"

This time it was Rawnie who smiled. "You think up that one all on your own?"

Adam shook his head. "Naw, I've got someone working 'round the clock thinking up witty remarks for me to use."

They'd dated briefly, nearly two months, until she found out what he did for a living and promptly dumped him.

"Sure is hot, huh?" Adam said, noticing Rawnie's caustic gaze had drifted over to the man seated beside him.

"Perhaps you should've reconsidered your present attire," Rawnie replied, flicking her eyes back on him.

Adam could tell, not just by Rawnie's expression (her upper lip was slightly curled), but also by her tone of voice and choice of words that her comment wasn't so much directed at the fact that he was wearing a suit on a very warm day as it was that he was wearing a designer suit and that right now she was probably imagining — and undoubtedly wanted him to imagine — the dozens of malnourished children forced to endure sixteen-hour days in Indonesian sweat shops just so he could wear this particular brand of labelled clothing.

"Yeah, I guess maybe I should have," Adam replied, noticing that the re-stitched, re-styled, slightly tattered blue jeans, handmade beige V-neck hemp shirt, and overworn sandals Rawnie was wearing made her look like the poster girl for thirdhand clothing, as though she should be in the display window of the nearest Goodwill or Salvation Army thrift store. "But the truth is, I really had no idea it was going to be this hot."

"Amazing how that could happen to someone who works in an air-conditioned office, lives in an air-conditioned condo, and drives an air-conditioned car," Rawnie said, not even attempting to disguise her sarcasm and then, when Adam nodded, admitting his guilt, she smirked and said, "We're a society of people so removed from our environment that we've become conditioned to dressing warmly in the middle of summer."

"Did you get that from a Greenpeace brochure?" Adam asked, smiling.

"You know something, I'd really love to stand here all day and do this, Adam, but I've got to be somewhere."

"On another TREPA mission?"

"No, actually, I'm on my way to an AA meeting," Rawnie replied, glaring at Adam before walking away.

"Nice to see you again," Adam called after her, smiling when she flipped him the finger over her shoulder.

To Be Continued . . .

ever-varying Madeline

Easing back into the patio chair, Adam took a long swig of his Diet Coke, set his glass down, and said, "Pardon the interruption. Where were we?"

"I believe I was telling you that my brother William has very unique tastes."

"Oh, yes," Adam said, his eyes tailing Rawnie and her friends as they made their way onto the patio at Smooth Herman's before returning his gaze to the man seated across from him, once again thinking the man was probably the strangest potential client he'd ever met. "Well, perhaps it might help if you were to describe your brother's tastes so I can get a better feel for what he's looking for."

"Fair enough," the potential client said, leaning forward slightly in his chair and clasping his hands together. "When it comes to women, my brother William is a card carrying member of the 'Variety is the vice of my life' club. Now, though I am certain if we conducted a poll we might discover women believe all men belong to this club, the truth is the average man is only capable of mild variances when it comes to the women he dates. He may, for instance, date a blond or a redhead instead of the usual brunette. He may develop an interest in Asian or Hispanic women instead of black women. He may even date women a little shorter or taller or heavier than he normally would. But rarely will he venture so far from his preferred type to cause people to stop and wonder, 'Oh my god, what is *he* doing with *her*?' This happens to William all the time. He is a connoisseur, a curator, of unique women."

Adam took a few moments to mull over what his potential client had just said. "And what is so unique about these women?"

The potential client smiled. "Perhaps taking advantage of Canada's position as the most culturally and ethnically diverse country in the world, several years ago he initiated a quest to date a variety of ethnic women possessing — hmmm, now, how shall I phrase this? Ethnic women possessing slight and perhaps not-so-slight aberrations in their physical make-up."

"What sorts of aberrations are we talking about here?"

"Hmmm, it's quite a list, actually," the potential client said, pausing momentarily to take a sip of his brandy. "To cite just a few: he has dated a Korean woman weighing over 350 pounds. A fifty-seven-year-old Jewish dwarf born the day Hitler committed suicide. A Pakistani woman with one eye. An Ecuadorian woman with a prosthetic hand. A Cambodian woman with no legs. And an anorexic Belgian woman whom he told me was 5'8" and weighed ninety-six pounds on their first dinner date and just a shade under ninety pounds on their third and final dinner date two weeks later."

"That's quite a list," Adam said. "And you weren't exaggerating. Your brother definitely has unusual tastes."

The potential client nodded. "He wasn't always like this. For most of his life he managed to keep himself under wraps, so to speak. It wasn't until our mother died that he let himself go, and his not-so-natural tendencies took over."

"I see," Adam said, picking up his Diet Coke and swirling the ice cubes around a few times in the glass. "But, to be honest, I still don't understand why you called my agency. It seems as though your brother isn't having difficulty finding a date."

The potential client started to speak, then stopped, started to speak again, again stopped, then, in a considerably lower voice said, "The truth is, William has taken a turn for the worse."

"Oh?"

"I believe he's become corrupted in his quest for the bizarre."

"How so?" Adam asked.

The potential client leaned forward. "He's considering . . . paedophilia," he whispered.

"Really?"

"Yes. But I'm certain that's all it is: a consideration. He's not a committed paedophile. He's really only considering it as part of his quest for the bizarre or maybe as a final chapter to his book."

"He's writing a book?"

The potential client nodded. "More of a diary, really. About his exploits."

"I see. And how much *material* does he have for this final chapter of his?"

"He's more or less doing research at this point."

"Which means?"

"Which means he's scouted a few possibilities, found someone he likes and . . ."

"And?"

"And this is why I'm here. I feel that if I don't redirect him or find a suitable replacement for his current *project*, he may end up in jail or worse."

The potential client downed a mouthful of brandy, leaving behind only a small sip in his tumbler. Adam motioned to the waitress to bring them another round.

"So how do you know about all this?"

"William was always quite willing to regale me with stories of his affairs with women," the potential client said, eyeing the remaining brandy in the tumbler. "At least once a month during the past two years, I would receive a call from him and he'd excitedly relate to me one of his Madeline adventures."

"Madeline adventures?"

After taking the final sip of his brandy, the potential client nodded and said, "He referred to all his dates as Madeline. He merely altered the title to reflect their physical aberration."

"For example?"

"For example, there was Madeline the Dwarf, Madeline the Elder, Madeline the Fag Hag, Madeline the Obese, Madeline the Legless. Always Madeline. Don't quote me on this, but I believe he got the name Madeline, as well as the idea of referring to them as such, from a Tennyson poem, where the narrator refers to his 'ever-varying Madeline.' Anyhow, although his desire for a particular Madeline was compelling, it usually only required a few dates with her for him to be completely sated and he'd go off in search of another. So, when I hadn't heard from him in a couple of months, I called to ask him how things were going and that's when I became suspicious."

"How come?"

"He told me he'd met someone but refused to give me any details about her. I tried for a week to get him to tell me who she was but he kept saying she was his secret. I probably should've guessed something was wrong when he didn't refer to her as Madeline."

Adam took a sip of his Diet Coke. "And so what exactly is it that you feel my agency might be able to assist you with?"

The potential client leaned forward again. "I believe that if we find William the right woman, it would take his mind off his current interest."

"What kind of woman are we talking about here?"

"Well, for one thing, she should be a woman. Someone at least over the age of twenty-one. Secondly, she should be the kind of woman who can sustain his interest for a long period of time. Someone able to stand up to him, who won't immediately fall victim to his charms or manipulations."

At that moment, the waitress came by to drop off their drinks and Adam took the opportunity to see if he could locate Rawnie. He spotted her standing with her two friends on the patio at Smooth Herman's. A few moments later, when she looked in his direction, he smiled and waved, wondering what her response was going to be this time.

. . . . To Be Continued . . .

still staring . . . .

"Who's that for?" Lance asked, pointing at Rawnie's raised middle finger.

"The guy I was talking to a few minutes ago," Rawnie replied, pointing in Adam's direction before turning her back on him.

"What's his deal, anyway?" Lucinda asked.

"He's suffering from sudden wealth syndrome."

Lance laughed. "Another trust-fund boy come of age?"

"No," Rawnie said, shaking her head. "He earned it the new-fashioned way. He won a lottery."

"Really?" said Lucinda, sounding intrigued. "How much?"

"A little over five million."

"Oh my God. Are you serious?"

Rawnie nodded. "He's one of our city's nouveau riche."

"What's he like?" Lance asked, coyly wrapping his tongue around the spout of his raspberry wine cooler.

"He's pretty much a jerk," Rawnie replied.

Lance sighed. "It's always the way."

"I wonder if he's more or less of a jerk now that's he's rich?" Lucinda asked.

"About the same. The only thing that's really changed since he won the money is he now drives a SAAB instead of a Sunfire and he started this supposedly avant-garde dating service."

"How do you know all this?"

"Because I . . . um, never mind. Not important. What were we talking about?"

"When?"

"Before I gave rich boy the finger."

"I think we were discussing Lucinda's boyfriend, Jeremy," Lance replied, "and how I think he's going to ask her to —"

"Oh, for Christ's sake," Rawnie said, interrupting Lance. "Can't you take a hint?"

"What?"

"He's still staring at me," Rawnie replied.

"Who?"

"Rich boy. Here," Rawnie said, shoving her strawberry daiquiri in Lucinda's direction. "Hold this for a second, please."

"What are you going to do?" Lance asked.

After Lucinda took her daiquiri, Rawnie struck the pose of a pissed-off gunfighter and gave Adam the finger with both hands while mouthing the words, "Get lost, loser."

. . . . **To Be Continued . . .**

and this won't bother you? . . . .

"How about Rawnie?" Adam said, taking his eyes off Rawnie and looking at his potential client.

"You mean, the woman you were speaking with a few minutes ago?"

Adam nodded. "I think she'd be the perfect woman for your brother."

"No offence," the potential client scoffed, "but she seems too . . . typical."

Adam chuckled. "Trust me, that gal is far from typical. Did you notice the clothes she was wearing? That's her Tuesday-Thursday-Saturday outfit. She has a Monday-Wednesday-Friday outfit and a Sunday outfit, as well. She got the idea from Einstein who wore the same suit every day so he wouldn't waste any mental energy deciding what to wear each day."

"Interesting."

"And she's full of secrets, too."

"Is that so? What sorts of secrets?"

"Well, on your way into the city, did you happen to notice the billboards?"

"I was meaning to ask you about that. Is it some sort of new advertising campaign?"

Adam leaned forward. "Rawnie did that."

The potential client frowned. "She painted all those big black X's?"

Adam nodded. "She's a member of this organization called TREPA. It's an acronym for The Real Environmental Protection Agency. Actually, she's the founder of it."

"Is that so?"

Adam nodded. "The main chapters are in Hamilton and Toronto but they have over ten thousand members worldwide now. They even have members in places as far away as Australia, Japan, India, and Nunavut."

"Are there annual membership dues?" the potential client asked, looking slightly amused.

Adam shook his head. "The only thing required to be a member is to do something for the Earth and have it verified by another source. And the emphasis is on doing something, not just slapping a 'Honk if you love the Earth' bumper sticker on your car or buying a 'Save the Rainforest' T-shirt, but actually going out there and actively challenging people's perceptions, trying to change the way they think."

"And marking up billboards with an 'X' qualifies as 'doing something'?"

"Well, that's not the only thing they do. She and some other members have put in speed bumps or 'Road Closed' barriers along really busy streets in Hamilton and Toronto. Or they'll repaint a one-way street and make it so there's one lane for cyclists, one for skateboarders and inline skaters, another one for pedestrians and the remaining lane for buses and emergency vehicles. Or they'll create a mini-park like they did last spring in Mississauga where they posed as a bunch of construction workers one night and actually went into a parking lot and planted a small tree in the middle of every parking space and then put up a sign at the gate that said, 'Lot Reserved For Trees, by order of TREPA.'"

"And how is it that you know all this about her?"

"We dated."

"Is that so?"

"Why do you think she's so hostile towards me?"

The potential client smiled. "And why is it you think Rawnie would be a suitable substitute for my brother's current project?"

"Well, it seems to me that even though the women your brother dates are quite unique, they still aren't that much of a challenge to him, right?"

The potential client nodded.

"Well, Rawnie would be a challenge. She would take months, maybe even years for him to get to know, let alone conquer. And she's definitely not someone he would get tired of after only a few dates."

The potential client picked up his tumbler of brandy. "Is there anything else worth knowing about this Rawnie woman," he said after taking a sip, "aside from her being an alcoholic?"

"A what?"

"She mentioned earlier that she was off to an AA meeting. I assumed she was an alcoholic."

Adam chuckled. "She was referring to me, I'm afraid."

"Oh, I'm sorry."

"No need to apologize. I've been sober for over a year now."

"Well, congratulations. Cheers," the potential client said, raising his tumbler.

"Thanks. And to answer your question, there's plenty more worth knowing about Rawnie. But I was thinking that maybe we should allow your brother to discover these things for himself."

The potential client nodded. "I suppose you're right."

"So, you're interested then?"

"I am. Where do we go from here?"

"Well, from here, it requires the down-payment we discussed over the phone. As soon as I receive it we'll begin making plans to put your brother in contact with Rawnie and —"

"And this won't bother you?"

"Excuse me?"

"Seeing my brother with this Rawnie woman?"

Adam shook his head. "Not at all. Why would it?"

"Well, you seem — how shall I put this — very much enamoured with her."

"Oh, for heaven's sake. You *can't* be *serious*!"

To Be Continued . . .

to be continued

"Sorry about that," George said to the two men seated at the table next to him. Then, turning to his wife, he said in a hushed voice, "There's no need to shout."

"Why not?" his wife replied, maintaining her loud voice. "What's left for me to do?"

George and Eileen had seen a marriage counsellor on Tuesday and this was their homework for the weekend: to do one thing the other wanted to do without question or complaint. Eileen's 'thing to do' was for her and George to sit out on a patio, have a drink and a conversation, do some people-watching, and maybe even meet some new people.

Since leaving their home on the East Mountain, George hadn't stopped complaining; complaining that Eileen had made him change his clothes to 'something more appropriate,' that they'd had to walk four blocks to Hess Village, that his back was sore, that they had to wait in line ten minutes to get into the Gown & Gavel, that they'd had to wait another ten minutes to get a table, that it was too hot outside on the patio, that the beer wasn't cold enough, that there were too many people on the patio, that there was too much noise. And now, after being seated for less than half an hour, he'd asked Eileen if she was ready to go home. To which she'd replied, "You *can't* be *serious*!"

"What do you want from me?" George said, shifting uncomfortably in his seat. "I agreed to do this, didn't I?"

"Yeah, and you've made me very aware that you've hated every second of it," Eileen replied before taking a sip of her piña colada.

"Besides, I think the whole point of us doing this is to try to enjoy the other person's activity."

"I am."

"No, you're not."

"How can you say that?"

"Because ever since we left the house you've been complaining. And now you want to leave."

"That's not —"

"I bet all you've been thinking about since we got in the car is how much you'd rather be at home watching sports."

That's all George did. All weekend, every weekend, since the twins — Cody and Cailey — moved out three years ago.

"That's not what I've been thinking."

"Really? Then what were you thinking?"

"I was thinking that it never used to bother you that I watched sports on the weekends."

"Of course it's bothered me."

"Well, why didn't you say something?"

"I shouldn't have to."

For years they'd promised each other that as soon as the twins were out of the house they'd spend their weekends doing the things they'd done before they'd had kids. Yet, since the twins departure three years ago, this was the furthest George had strayed from the couch on a Saturday.

"Why are you so upset?" George asked, moving forward slightly in his chair.

"You sure you want to know?"

George nodded.

"I'm upset because you're not the man I married."

"What are you talking about? Of course I am."

"No, George, you're not."

"What's so different?"

Glaring at him, Eileen made a quick comparison of the first three years of their marriage when they didn't have the twins and the last three when the twins were no longer at home. Well, for starters, she said to herself, you used to have more hair on your head and none on your back. You were fifty pounds lighter. And you didn't wear glasses. You also used to give me flowers once a month. And you used to have hobbies. Lots of them. You even used to play the sports you now only watch. You used to call the TV the 'Idiot Box' and wondered how anyone in their right mind could spend more than a few minutes watching it. Now who's the idiot? You also used to cook me dinner on Wednesdays and Sundays. Now I'm lucky if I can get you to order take-out once a month. You used to surprise me all the time with little gifts and poems and tell me you loved me at least twenty times a day. You used to want to explore every inch of Hamilton on foot. You used to have this incredible desire to —"

"Well?" George asked. "What's so different?"

"Never mind. It's too complicated," Eileen said, waving her hand at him. Then, after taking a sip of her piña colada, she sighed and said, "How did it come to this?"

"To what?"

"To us needing a marriage counsellor to tell us to do the things that used to come naturally to us?"

"Hey, seeing a marriage counsellor was *your* idea."

"Do you realize how embarrassed I was?"

"You? What about me?"

Eileen pushed her drink away from her. "What happened to us, George?" she said, tears suddenly welling in her eyes. "Where did we go wrong?"

"Hey, come on, things aren't that bad," George replied, reaching out to touch her arm.

"They're bad enough," Eileen snapped, pulling away from him and reaching into her purse to retrieve a tissue. "Oh, George, why don't we just get a —"

"Excuse me."

Eileen looked up to see a young couple standing on the other side of the cast-iron railing. One of them — the girl — was holding a camcorder. The other one — a young man — was holding a clipboard.

"Hi there," said the young man, reaching over the fence to shake Eileen's and George's hands. "We're going around Hamilton this weekend getting footage for a video to promote our city. Anyone who participates automatically qualifies for a chance to win some pretty amazing prizes."

"What's the catch?" George asked.

"No catch. We just get you to sign this consent form and then we give you a couple of minutes or so to tell us what it is you like about Hamilton. Then we submit the stories to our panel of judges and they decide who wins."

"A couple of minutes, huh?"

"Yes sir. Interested?"

"Sure," George said.

Eileen looked at George. "We are?"

"Where's the form?"

"It's right here," the young man said, handing George his clipboard. "The form basically states that you give us permission to film you and, if your footage is selected for the promotional video, permission to use it. You just print and sign your name at the bottom and I'll witness it."

"Sounds painless," George said, printing and signing his name on the form. "So, anything particular you're looking for?"

"Um, no, not really," the young man said, taking the form from George and signing it. "We're basically just looking for personal stories from Hamiltonians that might be of interest to a wider audience."

"Got the camera rolling yet?"

"We just have to film the release form with your signature on it to verify that it is you and then, okay, whenever you're ready you can start, sir."

After taking a moment to collect himself and then another to smile at Eileen, he looked directly into the camera and started talking.

"I came to Hamilton from Halifax in 1979. I'd just finished reading *My Country* by Pierre Berton and found myself inspired by a story about a couple of guys who decided to walk across Canada — from Halifax to Vancouver — just for the heck of it. I had a good job waiting for me in Vancouver that wasn't slated to start for another four months and so I thought, what the hell, I've got nothing better to do for the next little while and I started walking. On Day 74 I stopped. Not because of blisters or loneliness or because I ran out of money or I'd already arrived in Vancouver. I stopped walking because that was the day I set foot in Hamilton and discovered the love of my life. She was walking alone along The Bruce Trail on a Sunday afternoon, so lost in her own thoughts she didn't even notice me following her back to her home on Aberdeen Avenue. Nowadays, I suppose following a young woman home without her knowledge would be frowned upon. But at that time, it was perhaps a little more acceptable.

"Of course, even though I only had the clothes on my back and a couple hundred bucks to my name, I still had enough sense to realize that despite knowing where she lived, introducing myself to her in my current state probably would not garner me an invitation to come inside. And so I immediately checked into The Salvation Army, got myself cleaned up, and applied for various jobs around the city. The following week I was hired on a construction crew and used my first paycheque to rent a room in a very respectable, Victorian-styled home just off Aberdeen Avenue. My second paycheque was spent on some nice clothes, a haircut, and a bottle of cologne. And then, after watching her walking along the trail for three consecutive Sundays, I finally summoned the courage on the fourth Sunday to introduce myself, asking her, after she seemed not overly offended by my presence, if she'd like some company. She said yes and for the remainder of the afternoon and the rest of that summer, we explored the area in and around Hamilton on foot, hiking The Bruce Trail, Websters Falls, Spencer's Creek, The Devil's Punch Bowl, Cootes Paradise, The Waterfront, Red Hill Creek, Canteberry Hills, as well as all sorts of other places. Two years later, we were married at the very spot where we first met on The Bruce Trail and for our honeymoon we spent two weeks hiking around the city. Isn't that right, honey?"

Eileen smiled and nodded her head.

"Now," George said, after downing the last swig of beer in his glass. "I've heard of people living in Manhattan who never leave the island because it has everything they need to feel alive. I feel the same way about Hamilton. Sure I venture into Burlington and Dundas and Stoney Creek and Ancaster. I even get out to Toronto and Niagara Falls on occasion. But I've never been outside the city limits longer than a few days. And the reason for this is because Hamilton is, in my mind at least, a place of incredible beauty and inspiration. Of course, others might disagree. In some parts of Canada, Hamilton has a reputation as being primarily a steel town. But this is a bit of a misnomer as I'm certain anyone who spends some time in Hamilton will quickly discover for themselves. There are so many other aspects to this city. We have world-class golf courses and hotel accommodations. We have an internationally recognized university and art gallery. We have North America's oldest daily newspaper, the *Hamilton Spectator*. We have the most donut shops and Ph.D.'s per capita in Canada. We have the most waterfalls of any city in the world. We even have Canada's oldest farmer's market. And, of course, Hamilton is home to part of the Niagara Escarpment, which the UN has classified as a World Biosphere Reserve. So you see, Hamilton is much more than just a couple of big steel mills. In fact, when they held the World Cycling Championships here a while back, I had a chance to talk to dozens of people from all over the world — Brazil, Spain, Germany, Australia, France, England — and every single one of them couldn't stop talking about what a wonderful city Hamilton was."

At this point, George took his eyes off the camcorder lens. "Are my two minutes of fame up yet?"

"Um, yeah, I guess they are," the young man replied. "But, I mean, keep going if you want to. This is great stuff."

"Actually, I wouldn't mind getting another drink first if that's alright. My mouth is getting dry from all the talking. Would you like one, honey?"

Eileen nodded.

"Great. I'll be back in a minute," he said to Eileen and then, after getting up, he pointed his finger at the two young people and said, "To be continued," before walking quickly towards the side entrance of the Gown & Gavel.

"Did you get that?" the young man said, turning to the girl.

The girl nodded excitedly. "That was amazing."

"I know," the guy replied. Then, turning to Eileen, he said, "Is he your husband, ma'am?"

Eileen nodded.

"So, is that true, then?" the girl asked. "About him meeting you on The Bruce Trail like that?"

"Yes, it is," Eileen replied, smiling. What she wasn't sure was true was what had happened prior to their meeting on The Bruce Trail. George had never said anything about hiking from Halifax or having a job waiting for him in Vancouver. Nor had he ever mentioned staying at The Salvation Army or watching her for three consecutive Sundays before finally introducing himself. This was the first time she'd ever heard him speak of these —

"Well, that's by far the most interesting story I've heard," said the young man, interrupting her thoughts.

"Me too," replied the girl.

"Just out of curiosity," Eileen said, turning to the girl. "What does the winner get?"

"Um, well, the winner actually gets an all-inclusive weekend trip for two to —"

. . . . **To Be Continued . . .**

acknowledgements

Thanks to:

Jack David, for once again saying 'Yes.'

Jen Hale, new mother and editor extraordinaire, for another quick and painless editing process.

Nadine, Kulsum, Joy, Tania, Wiesia, Tracey, and Mary, for your patience, persistence, and invaluable assistance.

Arts Hamilton for selecting my first novel as 'Best Fiction Book' at the 2004 Annual Literary Awards; and all those who bought and/or read it.

Hamilton and Toronto for your inspiration.

The Leenders family, Milligan clan, and Paradigm gang, for your support.

And, a special thanks to my wife, Shannon, for your love, insights, and especially for bringing our little Mason man into the world! Je t'aime.

— Gordon j.h. Leenders

tobecontinued123@hotmail.com

SHANNON LEENDERS

Gordon j.h. Leenders holds degrees from McMaster University and Queen's University, works as a rehabilitation therapist in Hamilton, Ontario, and recently moved into a beautifully renovated schoolhouse with his wife Shannon, son Mason, and dog Brandi. His first novel, *May Not Appear Exactly As Shown*, was awarded the Best Fiction Book at the 2004 Annual Literary Awards by Arts Hamilton.

. . . . To Be Continued . . .

The stories continue in Volume Two
Spring 2006 . . .